Harlequin
romance
by Anne Mather
comes to life
on the movie screen

starring
KEIR DULLEA · SUSAN PENHALIGON

Leopard
in the
Snow

Guest Stars
KENNETH MORE · BILLIE WHITELAW

featuring GORDON THOMSON as MICHAEL
and JEREMY KEMP as BOLT

Produced by JOHN QUESTED and CHRIS HARROP
Screenplay by ANNE MATHER and JILL HYEM
Directed by GERRY O'HARA

An Anglo-Canadian Co-Production

OTHER
Harlequin Romances
by MARY WIBBERLEY

Many of these titles are available at your local bookseller,
or through the Harlequin Reader Service.

For a free catalogue listing all available Harlequin Romances,
send your name and address to:

HARLEQUIN READER SERVICE,
M.P.O. Box 707, Niagara Falls, N.Y. 14302
Canadian address: Stratford, Ontario, Canada N5A 6W4

or use coupon at back of books.

Original hardcover edition published in 1977
by Mills & Boon Limited

ISBN 0-373-02147-X

Harlequin edition published March 1978

PRINTED IN U.S.A.

Wild
Goose

by

MARY WIBBERLEY

Harlequin Books

TORONTO • LONDON • NEW YORK • AMSTERDAM • SYDNEY

CHAPTER ONE

'My dear Casey,' said Jack, 'you can't possibly travel to this place on your own. I wouldn't dream of letting you go.'

Casey didn't answer immediately. She was busily brushing her long honey gold hair in front of her hall mirror. Then she smiled. 'All right, what do you suggest?' She turned round to face her fiancé. 'Because I'm determined to go. Are you coming with me?'

'It's easy for you,' he grumbled. '*I* can't go hareing across Europe at the drop of a hat. I've a career——'

'And I haven't? That's what makes it so simple for me, don't you see? I'm twenty-three, love, not a child, and perfectly——'

'Yes, I know, perfectly capable. But you don't understand. Anything could happen——'

'I'm flying. And this *château* isn't in Siberia, it's in the South of France——'

'Yes, and a damned Russian living there——'

'About eighty, I imagine. After all, Great-Uncle Edward was. He's hardly likely to rape me——'

'I do wish you wouldn't be so coarse——'

Casey burst out laughing. 'Don't be stuffy! The sooner we get to Parker, Parker, Fenwick and Parker, the better. They'll tell us all about it. So please stop worrying.' She reached up to kiss his cheek.

'And if we don't go now, we'll be late.'

A last quick look round her flat, picking up her handbag from the settee as she did so, and Casey went out, followed by Jack. She looked at him as they went down in the lift, and gave a small invisible sigh. He was so proprietorial at times. She knew it was solely because he was concerned about her welfare, but she was independent enough to resent it, to make her want to shock him—as she had so nearly done, moments before. He caught her glance, and smiled at her. 'I'll be coming in the office with you?'

'Of course. It concerns you nearly as much as it does me, doesn't it? After all, we are getting married next year——'

'This week, if I had my way.' The corner of his mouth twitched.

'Please don't let's go over that now. You know I can't be rushed,' she began.

'Mmm, I sometimes wonder if you really love me——'

'Of course I do!' Her eyes widened in surprise, but laughter wasn't far away.

He caught her hand. 'Then marry me now—and we'll honeymoon in the damned place if that's what you want.'

Casey pulled her hand away gently. 'Sometimes, sir, I wonder if it's me or my *château* you're after——'

'Huh, you want to sell the place. It'll be a liability—nothing else. You don't even know what condition it's in. It could be a mouldering old ruin——'

'But I intend to look for myself. See? Now we're back to square one.'

They left the lift, and crossed the entrance hall of the block of luxury flats where Casey lived, and the grey-uniformed doorman saluted them.

'Morning, miss. Want your car?'

'No, thanks, Dobbs, we're going in Mr Sutherland's.'

They went out into the warm sunshine of a June day. The roar of London's traffic came distantly, muted by the tall trees of the square in front of the flats. Five minutes later they were in the thick of it, wending their way down Oxford Street towards the solicitors.

'So you see, Miss Cantrell,' said Mr Parker, pursing his lips slightly and looking at Casey over gold-framed pince-nez, 'it is indeed advisable for you to go and see the Château Fleuron as soon as it can be managed. As far as we know, it's habitable—but—' a gentle shrug, implying no responsibility on his part, 'one never knows in these matters, especially when they're abroad.' He too managed to give the impression that the place might be in Siberia. Casey kept her face straight. She was calm, easy-going—but with a determined streak.

'I know. I intend going as soon as I can,' she answered. 'In fact Mr Sutherland was only saying this morning that he'd like to come with me if he could manage it.'

'Yes,' Mr Parker looked relieved. 'You see, Mr Borodinov is an—ahem—unknown quantity. We know little about him save that Mr Cantrell left the *château* to be equally divided between the two of you——'

'What!' Jack stood up in agitation. He turned accusingly to Casey. 'You never told me anything about sharing it with this Russian fellow——'

'I forgot,' she said simply. It was the truth. She looked at Jack, annoyed at his outburst. 'What does it matter? I should imagine it's big enough to be divided quite easily——'

'That's not the point.' Jack subsided unhappily on to his chair. He disliked losing control of any situation, and he just had. Probably, thought Casey, he won't be able to eat any lunch now.

'Yes, well,' continued Mr Parker, rustling the papers before him, 'we will give you a note, of course, to take to the French *notaires* in Cannes—French law is slightly different from ours, of course'—he smiled gently and it was quite clear what *his* opinion of French law was—'and everything, we hope, will be straightforward. I'm sure there will be no difficulties about selling your half share to Mr Borodinov should you——'

'Oh, but I don't,' Casey interrupted. 'I've no intention of selling anything. Uncle Edward wanted me to have half of his *château*, and that's precisely what I'm going to have.' She gave both of the men in the office with her a quiet, sweet smile. They both looked at her, then at each other. No words were needed. Jack knew the smile of old. So did Mr Parker. The only thing left to do was change the subject, which Casey did.

'Do you know anything at all about Mr Borodinov?' she asked.

'His full name'—Mr Parker consulted a paper on his desk—'Igor Aleksandrovich Borodinov, he's Russian, he's known and worked with your great-uncle Edward for the past ten years, and two years ago went to the Château Fleuron to live, taking with him a man-servant called Boris, whose surname we don't appear to have. Your uncle was in failing health by this time, of course, being in his late seventies, and by all accounts Mr Borodinov looked after him'—he paused at Jack's ill-concealed snort, looked up, saw that he wasn't about to say anything, and continued—'until he died six months ago. That, Miss Cantrell, is as much as I can tell you.'

Casey looked evenly at Jack. She could almost have read his mind at that moment. She would get his full opinion of Russians over their lunch. And especially what he thought about ones who were on the spot when wealthy, elderly and eccentric recluses died.

'Thank you, Mr Parker,' she stood up. 'You've been extremely helpful. I shall be going next week, I've decided. I'll phone you before then, of course, and call in to collect any necessary papers.' They shook hands and were ushered out of the inner sanctum by a secretary.

Jack waited until they were outside before venting his feelings. 'That does it,' he said. 'You're definitely not going alone!'

She looked at his tight features. 'You mean you're going to be able to get time off to go with me?'

'I'll jolly well make time, don't worry. I'm due for three weeks, I'll have a word with the boss——'

'But all those plans for the marvellous skyscrapers that are going to change the face of London—you can't drop jobs in the middle, not a busy architect like you,' she said innocently.

He looked sharply at her, as if trying to detect sarcasm. 'I'll have to take the work with me. Most of it's already well enough advanced for that. And why didn't you tell me?'

'Tell you what?'

'You know damned well! That you'd only got half of this damned place——'

'Because I forgot.' Casey was losing patience rapidly. 'And please stop referring to it as "this damned place." It's a *château*, it's half mine, and I'm looking forward to seeing it.' She shook her arm free of his. 'And I intend to enjoy my lunch, so stop sulking.'

He came to a halt, there on the busy pavement, causing passers-by to swerve. The crowds milled round them as they stood facing each other.

'I'm not sulking.'

'It looks remarkably like it to me.'

There came one of his swift changes of mood she now knew so well. He managed to look contrite, suddenly boyish—and very charming.

'Sorry, love. I've been working so damned hard lately—I shan't say another word about anything. We're going to enjoy our lunch. Okay?' The Sutherland grin was back in place.

'Okay.' She took his arm again. 'I'm starving. Let's go!'

But later that night, as Casey prepared for bed in her flat, she thought about the day, and in particular about Jack. She loved him, but she had many doubts about him, which was why she was in no hurry to rush to the altar. She knew that she herself had a strong character—as he had. And when she married, it would be for life. Therefore, everything must be right. Until all her minor fears about marriage were overcome, she would be patient. As he must learn to be. She sighed as she turned down the covers of the bed. Just lately, Jack had changed, become more eager—too eager—to be married. If only he'd learn, she thought as she slid between the cool sheets, that he can't rush me, that I panic because I've seen too many marriages go wrong, then we might do better. She lay down, tired, and into her mind drifted the picture of an elderly Russian with a fierce beard and staring eyes. She smiled to herself. Poor Jack! He'd already got Igor Borodinov tabbed as some kind of Rasputin, when in fact he would probably turn out to be a gentle old man. They would soon know, within a week, in fact, and then she would be able to decide what to do about the Château Fleuron. One thing was certain, she thought, as she began to drift easily into sleep. No one, not even Jack, was going to rush her into any decision she might regret.

CHAPTER TWO

THEY were nearly there. Despite her calm exterior, a few dozen butterflies clamoured for space in Casey's stomach and she took a deep breath and looked at Jack beside her driving the hired Renault, his eyes busily concentrating on the narrow track winding upwards ahead of them. She passed her tongue over lips that had suddenly gone dry.

'I'm scared,' she confessed, forcing a little laugh.

'So am I.' But there was no humour in his voice, and she felt no better, worse if anything. She took out her lipstick and gazed in the mirror on the sunshield at the top of the windscreen. 'You won't need that,' his voice came, even though he hadn't looked round. 'He'll be too old to appreciate feminine wiles.'

'But I'll feel good,' she retorted, annoyed. It might have been better had she come alone. If Jack was going to be prickly like this, they would end up having a row—and that she didn't need. She sighed, steadied her hand, and looked at herself in the glass. Her wide grey eyes stared back at her, sooty-lashed, and her full soft mouth trembled ever so slightly. She lifted her chin. Damn you, she thought, not sure whether she meant the stony-faced Jack or the unknown Russian at the *château*. And where on earth was it? They should be nearly within sight of it now. The directions from a man in the village below had been quite explicit. Then she realised partly why Jack was in a bad humour. It was not only their destination, it was the fact that in the village she had had to do all the talking, ask all the questions, because she spoke French fluently, and he not a word. She put the lipstick on with a defiant flourish, then rubbed her lips together. And Jack disliked it when he wasn't in perfect control of any situation. Which is hardly anything to blame me for, she thought. It's not my fault that you only speak English.

'They said there was a sharp turn right any time now,' she said quietly, 'then up the path and we'll see a wall——'

'Okay, you already told me that. I'm looking. I know what I'm doing.'

She put her lipstick away and let out her breath slowly. Just for a moment she hoped Igor Borodinov would be as Rasputin-like as Jack feared. It would serve him right. The image conjured up restored her good humour and she looked out of the window so that he wouldn't see her smile. There was a high dry stone wall to their right, and it effectively concealed any land that lay behind it. Lush trees grew everywhere, and flowers and shrubs seemed to live in the very wall itself. The air was hot, the sun high in the sky, and through the open windows they could hear the birdsong, and her heart lifted. Old ruin or not, the Château Fleuron could hardly have a more beautiful setting. They had been climbing steadily since leaving the village, and when she looked back she could see the Mediterranean far away, glittering greenly in the sunlight.

He swung the car sharply right, and they began bumping up another, even narrower track, though it seemed impossible that anything could be narrower than the one they had just left.

'This won't do the springs any good,' Jack growled. Casey, hanging on to the back of her seat as they jerked and jolted their way up, silently agreed. She was about to tell him so when she saw the higher wall, crumbling in places, looking as if it might collapse on them at any second, then a gap in it—'Stop the car. Look!' she exclaimed.

He stopped; they looked. It was there, in the distance behind the wall, surrounded by trees, tall, turreted, of grey stone that glittered in the sun—most unmistakably a *château*, and quite beautiful, although ancient, with grey pantiled roofs and dozens of windows. Even Jack was impressed. 'My God!' he said reverently.

It had dignity. That was, she thought, the perfect way to describe it if you had to do it in one word. Dignity. It stood there proudly, as it had done for centuries, and it was no ruin. Whatever it might be like inside, it was solid and impressive-looking from where they sat. And it's mine, she thought. Well, half mine anyway. At that moment it didn't seem to matter.

They drove on, and the gateway was the second surprise. Jack came to a halt outside it before turning in, and gave a long low whistle. Two tall stone pillars supported lions' heads, also in stone, and wrought iron gates were wide open. A dusty drive wound its way along to vanish in the trees, and Casey touched his arm. 'Let's go,' she said.

He looked at her. 'They certainly knew how to build in those days,' he remarked.

'Didn't they just.' His mood had changed, which was a relief. He turned in and they drove slowly along, and a minute later, there came the third surprise. After the trees came wild untended lawns, but nearer the *château*, which they could now see, and it looked even more impressive the closer they went, were several greenhouses, to one side, and rows of vegetables growing alongside them. A man stood there, some distance away on Casey's side of the car. A big man, wearing tattered jeans and nothing else, holding a spade, digging away. He paused in his task and looked briefly at them. For an instant, Casey's eyes met his before he bent to his spade again, and she experienced a shock of awareness. He ignored them, concentrating on his task, and for a moment, before Jack spoke, she observed him unnoticed. Even from the distance she could see that he was built like an ox. Huge powerful shoulders and arms, well over six feet in height, and with black curly hair. His face she could no longer see, but she wanted to . . .

'I'll bet that's Boris,' said Jack. 'Somehow I imagined a doddery old manservant.'

'So did I,' agreed Casey thoughtfully. Where on earth had she seen him before?

Then he was out of sight, hidden by the green-houses, and they reached the front entrance. A massive wooden door stood open beyond some worn steps, and inside was the glimpse of a shadowy hall. Slamming the car door shut, Casey and Jack stood for a moment looking, and he looked at her.

'Well, we're here,' he said. 'Now to meet your fellow owner.'

Casey caught his hand. 'Jack—wait,' she said. 'Please —be nice.'

He lifted a mocking eyebrow. 'My dear girl, I shall be charm itself,' he answered smoothly. 'You know me.'

I do, she thought. Oh, yes, I do. And that's why I'm worried. There was no sense in antagonising the elderly Russian the moment they arrived. Then she saw him, and a sense of relief washed over her. It was going to be all right.

Standing there in the doorway was an elderly man all right—but no Rasputin. A kindly-faced man, with white hair—no fierce beard at all, just kindly blue eyes that looked at them as he came forward and gave them a little bow.

'Hello,' Casey held out her hand as she went up the steps to meet him. 'I'm Casey Cantrell.'

'Hello,' he shook her hand, and a smile lit his eyes. 'You are most welcome. Please to come inside.' He looked gently, enquiringly at Jack.

'My fiancé, Jack Sutherland,' she said quickly.

'How do you do.' His English was heavily accented,

but he spoke it perfectly. The two men shook hands, and Casey watched Jack's face. Pleasant, controlled, yet there was a speculative look about it that she knew of old. But for now, all was well.

'Please to follow me. There is food ready for you.' He turned and led the way into the hall, leaving them to follow. 'Your journey was good?'

'Very pleasant, thanks.' She looked about her. There would be so much time later to see everything properly, but the first impression was of space and light and coolness. All the walls were of stone, the floor as well, and a high stone fireplace dominated one wall, ornately carved, set with logs ready to be lit. Casey sighed. She had pictured so many things, but reality is always a little different.

'I have set you a meal in the kitchen,' the old man said, taking them down a stone corridor. Their footsteps echoed along the hard stone floor. Pictures hung on the walls, and it didn't take an expert to see that they were valuable. Some of these, too, were part of her inheritance, and they would need to reach agreement on them. But not now.

The kitchen was a further surprise. Huge, high-ceilinged, but with a modern cooker and cupboards—and two large alsatians lying watching them by the window. The Russian spoke to them, then turned to Casey and Jack. 'I am telling them that you are welcome here,' he said. 'They will not touch you. They are very good guard dogs, but very obedient. Please sit down—unless you would like to wash first?'

Casey sat at the table. 'No, thanks,' she answered. 'We washed at the airport.'

'I will,' said Jack, 'if you don't mind.'

'Of course. Come this way.' Casey was left alone, and she looked across at the dogs, who regarded her unblinkingly. As her host returned, alone, she said:

'It's very kind of you, Mr Borodinov, to have a meal ready——' she stopped as he began to chuckle. Surely she had said nothing amusing?

'Ah, no, excuse me, Miss Cantrell, I am not Mr Borodinov. My name is Boris—I am the manservant here. Mr Borodinov is my—what is the word? My boss.'

Casey stared at him, stunned. 'Forgive me,' she said. 'But I—I thought——' she stopped, too bewildered to speak.

He smiled. 'A natural mistake. I greeted you at the door. I should have said who I was. It is I who should beg your forgiveness. Mr Borodinov is busy outside.'

Then she knew. Casey cleared her throat. 'We saw someone near the greenhouses, digging, as we came in.' She had to pause to swallow. 'I don't suppose——'

'Yes, it was he. He loves the garden, and I am too old.' He smiled. 'He grows the food, I cook it.'

'Oh, I see.' Then Jack returned. Casey plunged in, before she could give herself time to think. Because one thing she knew. Jack also thought that Boris was Igor Borodinov. The only snag was—what would his reaction be? 'This is Boris, Jack,' she said. 'Mr Borodinov was the man we saw in the garden.'

The atmosphere became noticeably different. Jack's eyes met hers, and her heart lurched. But all he said was: 'I see.'

Boris looked from one to the other. 'Now please, sit down, and I will serve your meal. A little wine for you both?'. Whatever were his private thoughts, his hospitality was not to be faulted. He poured them wine, then went over to the cooker. A few minutes later they were eating a delicious roast chicken and vegetables.

Sitting in a quiet room overlooking the gardens, Casey sipped her hot coffee. She was alone. Jack had gone with Boris to carry the cases upstairs to their rooms, and she had told them she would go up later. She needed to think, and to do so, had to be alone. Everything had changed, so subtly—Jack most of all. It was as if he had taken it personally that Boris was not Igor Borodinov—and because she was tired from their long journey, she didn't for the moment know how to cope. She stood up and went over to the window, and looked out. She could see the greenhouses, but of the tall well-built man, there was no sign. He hadn't stopped, hadn't come in to greet them. Perhaps— she caught her breath. Perhaps he didn't want *them.* It was a new, disturbing thought to have. Things worked both ways.

There was a faint sound at the door, and she turned, to tell Jack what she thought—and a man walked in. Not Jack, not Boris. The big man from the garden outside, the Russian with whom she shared her *château.*

For a moment he stood inside the doorway looking at her, and she saw him clearly for the first time, and a pulse beat in her throat at the sight of him. He was a giant of a man, built like an athlete, tall, muscular and hairy—naked from the waist up—and barefoot. But it was his face that she found herself unable to tear her eyes from. For Igor Borodinov was devastatingly attractive. Not in a conventional way—he was too tough for that. High cheekbones, a hard square chin, wide mouth and deep brown eyes, almost black eyes under thick, faintly slanting eyebrows, a nose that was straight—and black hair that was short and curly. And whether he knew it or not—and it might be that he was not consciously aware of it—one thing struck her quite unmistakably. He didn't want Casey there. He looked across the room at her, surveying her coolly from those deep brown eyes, then walked slowly towards her.

'Miss Cantrell?' he said. His voice was deep, the Russian accent pronounced. 'I am Igor Borodinov.' He held out his hand and she took it, hiding a wince at the sheer strength of his grip.

'How do you do.' Something about him stung her. His manners might be impeccable—which fact she doubted, or he would surely have taken the trouble to put some clothes on before greeting her—but his air of rejection was everwhelming. 'We saw you in the garden on our way up,' she smiled.

'Yes?' There was nothing to indicate that he had seen them. 'I was busy growing food. There is much work to be done here.' Irrationally she wished that Jack were there with her. But he was no doubt trying to find out all he could from Boris about her co-owner —while the same co-owner was busily making it clear that she wasn't really welcome. Her hackles rose. She possessed an even, happy temperament, but when she sensed injustice, her other self took over. Her eyes narrowed.

'I'm sure there is,' she said. 'And now that I'm here, I'm sure we will be able to come to some arrangement about that.'

He lifted one eyebrow fractionally. 'Arrangement? I am not sure what you mean. You wish to do some gardening, perhaps?'

I'm going to hit you in a minute, she thought. Good and hard. And the thought shocked her, because violence was not in her nature. But never before had she met a man for whom she felt such instant—and undoubtedly mutual—antipathy. It was an almost tangible sensation, like waves of current in the room, an anti-magnet pushing them apart.

'Hardly,' she said coolly. Whatever happens, hold on to your temper. Lose that, and you're lost. 'But now that you and I own half the *château* each,' she laid a gentle emphasis on that last word, 'I'm sure we should find some way of sharing the maintenance of it.'

'You are intending to live here?' She looked at him, tempted most deliciously to say yes, if only to see the shock on his face.

'I don't know,' she compromised. 'I haven't seen round it yet, though I'm sure I will soon. Then I'll decide.' It was his turn for the narrowed eyes, the shrewd look.

'I see. Please—sit down and finish your coffee. We have much to discuss.'

'My fiancé is with me,' said Casey. 'Perhaps we had better do it when he comes in.'

'Why? Does he decide things for you?' The bluntness of his words took her by surprise, and she felt her cheeks redden.

'Certainly not,' she snapped. 'I make up my own mind——'

'Then it should not be necessary to wait. I prefer to speak to you.' He sat down opposite her. 'I will be brief, Miss Cantrell. I would like to buy your half of the *château* from you——'

They hadn't heard the door open. Not until Jack spoke did they realise he was in the room. 'That's the most sensible thing I've heard today,' he said, and walked in.

There was an electric moment of silence, then Igor Borodinov rose to his feet and held out his hand. The two men faced each other, Casey watching them. Igor was taller by several inches than Jack, who was six feet himself, and well built. But against the other man he looked almost puny. They shook hands, and she could almost see the subtle assessing, like a pair of strange dogs who meet, weigh each other up, and then decide whether or not to fight.

'Jack Sutherland—Mr Borodinov,' said Casey mechanically.

As they shook hands, the Russian said: 'Please call me Igor. I think my other name is rather difficult.' He looked at Casey, the brief handshake over.

'Yes, thank you.' The atmosphere had, incredibly enough, eased slightly. She could almost see the humour in the fact that these two appeared to be allies, however unwilling. They both wanted her to sell. The only snag was, she had absolutely no intention of doing so. 'And you must call me Casey.'

He bowed slightly. 'But of course. Casey—that is an unusual name, is it not?' Was he actually trying to be polite?

'My name's Katherine—my initials are K.C.,' she explained patiently, then added, taking much pleasure in doing so: 'It was my Uncle Edward who first gave me the nickname, when I was a child, and it stuck.'

'I see. Of course. Now that you have had some dinner, perhaps you would like a drink?' He moved across the room to a sideboard in the corner by the window, and opened one of the cupboards. He didn't walk, she decided, he loped. He was like some powerful animal who shouldn't be caged indoors. She suddenly felt a frisson of fear down her spine. He looked like a man who always got what he wanted. She glanced at Jack, to see him watching the Russian, hard-eyed, and for the first time, she felt glad that he was with her. Even if he did want her to sell as well.

'Vodka—cognac—kirsch? I am afraid we have not

a big selection, but I drink very little, and Boris not at all.'

'Kirsch, please,' said Casey, and watched him pour it into a liqueur glass.

'Vodka for me,' said Jack. 'Any lime or orange?'

'Of course. Excuse me a moment.' He handed Casey her glass and went out. After the door had closed, Jack looked at her.

'Wow, he's a cool one,' he said.

'What do you mean?' She knew, but she wanted to hear it from him.

He pulled a face. 'He doesn't waste time, does he?'

'If you mean by asking me to sell, no, he doesn't,' she agreed. 'And he doesn't want us here either. He's made that perfectly clear.' She slowly sipped at the sharp white liqueur. 'But there's not much he can do about it.'

'Well, you'll have to make up your mind soon. One thing's sure—I'm not going and leaving you here with him.' He said it very flatly, and Casey began to smile.

'Why do you say that?' But she already knew.

'You shouldn't need me to tell you,' he answered, and his mouth had a certain set to it. 'He probably eats girls like you for breakfast.'

'Don't be ridiculous! He looks quite——'

'Come off it! You're not that naïve,' he snapped. 'I shouldn't think any woman's safe when he's around.'

She burst out laughing. 'I do believe you're jealous!'

'You know damned well I'm not.' But he was angry, Casey could tell. She would normally have tried to

soothe him, but her own nerve ends were ragged after all that had happened. Not only that, Jack's idea was preposterous. He hadn't seen the way Igor had looked at her when he came into the room. Had he done so, he would have known without a doubt that the Russian found her not in the slightest degree desirable. And that, she realised a second later, was as almost positively insulting as his subtle unwelcome had been. But she wasn't prepared to work out precisely why she should think so.

A few minutes later Igor returned bearing a jug of orange juice. She watched him, assessing Jack's remarks as he poured out the drinks. Vodka and orange for Jack, orange juice for himself. Jack had been looking at him through a man's eyes, his summing up had been instant. And now, glancing casually at him, Casey admitted what she had denied to herself before. The vibrations hadn't all been of sheer antagonism. Some other quality had been there—and now she knew what it was. The Russian possessed an animal magnetism that could not be ignored. It was there in the way he moved, the leashed strength, the eyes—those eyes that suddenly met hers as she watched him, and it was like a physical shock, for it was as if he knew, he knew.

She couldn't look away. His eyes held her. Then he smiled slowly, and spoke, voice deep and accented. 'The kirsch is to your liking, Casey?' he asked.

'Yes, thank you.'

He held up his glass. '*Na zdorovye*—your health.'

Then he looked at Jack. 'Is the vodka all right?'

'Fine, thanks.' Jack was restless. He walked over to the window and looked out to where it was rapidly going dark. 'We'd like to look around, when convenient.'

'But of course. This evening?'

'Perhaps tomorrow might be better,' Casey interrupted. She didn't mind Jack taking charge occasionally, but if both of them were being awkward, she intended letting them know—and she was was very good at doing things her own way when she chose—that they weren't going to make her decisions for her. 'I'm rather tired, and besides, I would think it's easier to look around in the daytime.' She gave Igor a pleasant smile.

'As you wish.' He regarded her with a level glance. 'If you will excuse me then, I have more work to do outside.'

'In the dark?' Casey asked, faintly amused. It seemed to her a very transparent excuse to get away.

'That is the only time to water the vegetables in this part of the world—when the sun has gone,' he answered. 'Boris will be in the kitchen if you want him.' He walked out and left them alone.

Jack came back from the window, jingling the change in his pockets. 'I think we can consider ourselves told off—in the nicest possible way, of course,' he said, but he didn't seem displeased. Casey looked stonily at him.

'All right, Jack, point taken.' She jumped to her feet.

'He's an arrogant beast, I don't know about anything else.'

'Just wait till you see the rooms he's given us,' Jack said. 'I don't think they could be further apart if he'd tried. Mine's at the end of a long corridor up a flight of stairs, so you're quite safe from *me*. Trouble is—are you safe from *him*?'

'I don't think you're funny,' she answered, exasperated.

'I wasn't trying to be,' he said. 'Just telling you.'

'And now you have. I'm tired, I'm going to tell Boris I'd like a bath—always supposing there are bathrooms here.' She went towards the door, and Jack picked up a magazine from a pile by the window.

'I'll study this,' he said, 'while you're gone. I might learn some French, who knows?' He sat down and opened it. Casey sighed, and went out.

Two prickly men is what I can well do without, she thought. Thank goodness for Boris, I can't imagine him being moody or aggressive.

She thought that she knew exactly where the kitchen was. The only trouble was, she admitted to herself a few moments later—she had somehow got lost in a maze of corridors and doors, And all looking the same. She stood there feeling slightly foolish, debating whether or not to retrace her steps to the sitting room where Jack was, or to try again. There was a staircase nearby, and the next moment she heard footsteps, and waited. But it wasn't Boris who came down, it was Igor. Fully dressed—at least, he had put a shirt and sandals on. He slowed down as he saw her, then came over to her. Close to, he was even taller than she had remembered.

'You wish something?' he enquired.

'Yes. I was looking for the kitchen and Boris,' she answered. 'Only I seem to be lost.' Let him laugh if he dared.

But he didn't laugh. 'I see. It's that way.' He pointed, then hesitated. 'He may be out with the dogs now. Can I help you?'

'Is there a bathroom? I'd like a bath if possible.'

'Yes. Come, I will show you. The method of plumbing is old-fashioned. This way.' He turned and ran up the stairs again, and she followed him. Up and up, along another twisting corridor—then he opened a door. A gargantuan bathtub sat squarely in the centre of an enormous room. Oh, God, she thought, it'll take an ocean to fill that. She looked at it in dismay, visions of wallowing in hot scented water receding rapidly.

'Thank you. Er—is my room near here? Only I need my things.'

'Yes. Come.' Leaving the door open, he walked further along, opened another door, and stood waiting outside it. She saw her case by a large bed. Casey sighed a little sigh.

'Thanks, I'll manage now.' But he didn't move away. He stood there looking at her, and Casey felt herself go warm. She didn't know why he should have this effect on her—except perhaps Jack's words were too well remembered. She took a step into the room, to let him know he wasn't needed—and then he spoke.

28

'One moment, please.'

'Yes?' Why didn't he *go*? She didn't like being alone with him.

'A question. Forgive me if I seem impertinent, but I must ask it.'

She swallowed. 'What is it?' She was prepared for anything—except what came next. And for one stunning moment she thought she mustn't have heard correctly.

'Are you and Jack lovers?'

Dumbfounded, she stared at him, unable to look away. Then she found her voice. 'What did you say?'

He repeated it. There had been no mistake. There came a moment's electric silence, then she burst out: 'How *dare* you!' Her cheeks flamed.

'I ask it for a reason——'

'Then you have no right at all!' she flared. She swung away from him and he caught her arm. His fingers were like steel.

'Wait.'

'Take your hands off me at once, and get out of my way——' she put her hand on his fingers and tried to pull them away, and he released her. She was shaking with sudden, overwhelming—and frightening—rage. 'Leave me alone!' She whirled round to face him.

He didn't move, and that was more frightening still. He seemed completely impervious to her anger. 'I ask only for this reason—nothing else. The dogs are allowed to roam the castle freely at night. Do you not understand what I am saying?'

Then, suddenly, she did. She closed her eyes, weakened by her outburst. 'You mean——'

'I mean if either of you were to leave your rooms, it could be dangerous for you. Your way of life concerns me not at all.'

She swallowed hard. Very calmly she answered: 'Then you don't need to warn me. I sleep alone. Does that answer your question?' She lifted her chin, spirit fast returning. He had done it deliberately, she felt sure, but there was no way of proving it, yet suddenly she wanted to anger him equally. He nodded.

'Not that it's any of your business anyway,' she said sharply. 'And it's a pity you didn't ask Jack—or were you frightened you might have got a more direct answer—like a punch on the jaw?' Her eyes flashed her contempt. Then he smiled—quite gently, but her scalp prickled.

'Perhaps,' he agreed, more amused than anything else, apparently. 'But I have asked you, have I not? And English girls don't go around giving men punches on the jaw——'

'There's always a first time——'

'But not, I think, from you.'

'You don't know me at all,' she began—but he stopped her.

'But yes, I think I do. Your uncle told me much about you—about his visits to you in England over the past years, when you were younger. I know much about you. Which is why I did not think my question would give offence. You are, after all, much travelled, no? And old enough to know what life is about—but you reacted like a child when I spoke——'

'I think,' she cut in, 'you've said enough——'

'No, I haven't. I haven't even begun to say what I wish to say, nor why I wish to buy this *château* from you. And on that subject I will talk privately with you —not with him.' He stopped.

Casey was getting mad again. She could feel it. 'Jack's my fiancé,' she said. 'We're going to be *married* —and share everything.'

'No,' he said quietly, 'I don't think so.'

'I beg your pardon?' He certainly knew how to come out with the unexpected. Casey stared hard at him, unbelieving.

'I do not think you will get married to him. He is not suitable for you.'

CHAPTER THREE

FOR a few moments Casey was too flabbergasted to even attempt to speak. The whole scene was like some bad dream, and growing worse. This man, this perfect stranger, a big scruffy-looking Russian with the manners of a bear, was calmly standing there and telling her that *he* didn't think Jack was suitable for her. Worse, he was saying the words with a devastating calmness—almost as if they were discussing nothing more important than the weather. I'm going mad, she thought. But it was all real enough.

She found her voice. 'And who the hell do you think you are to dare to speak to me like that?' her lips quivered with the leashed tension inside her.

'You know who I am. I have offended you? But why should——'

'Yes, you damn well have! In fact, you're the most offensive ill-mannered man I've met in a long time, and that's saying something. I suggest you keep your personal opinions to yourself in future——'

He began to laugh, a deep laugh of genuine amusement—and that did it. Casey hit him as hard as she could, right across his face. Incensed, too mad to care what she had done, she blurted out: 'Now laugh that off!'

The mark on his cheek went red, and he put his

hand up. Then he looked down at her. But he made no move to touch her—and the laughter had finished. 'So,' he said, and it was very softly indeed. 'So, you have the fire in you after all. It is good for a woman to have spirit——'

'I don't need you to tell me what I should have, thank you,' she retorted smartly, 'any more than you'd like me to stand here discussing your personality. Though I could have a lot to say on that subject if I got going.'

'Really? You intrigue me. Please go on——'

'Well, for a start, you pretended you hadn't seen us come up to the *château*, and you had. But you didn't bother to come in, not for ages afterwards, and when you did, you made it quite clear we weren't welcome here, and then'—she had to pause for breath—'you plunge straight in and ask me to sell my half of the *château*—just like that, when I've not even been here five minutes——' she paused, fully launched on the subject but not sure what other crimes he had committed.

'Is that all?' he enquired politely, and it was difficult to tell if he were amused or angry, so dark and shadowy was it where they stood.

'No, it's not all. If you'd any manners you'd have put some clothes on before coming in!' she finished.

'Ah, good. Now you have said it all, perhaps?'

'Yes.' She didn't know what was the matter with her; if Jack, or any of her friends for that matter, could have heard her, they would not have known her. She had never spoken to anybody thus before. Yet it was as if she could not stop.

'And you feel better for having said all these things. Now I suggest you go and have your bath. Before you do, I did not pretend I had not seen you drive up. I saw you very well—I did not see any reason to rush in, for Boris was awaiting your arrival, and my own tasks were more important.' He paused. 'And as for me making it clear you were not welcome—I was not aware that I was doing so.' She saw the flicker of his half smile in the shadowy darkness. 'Perhaps you are more perceptive than I thought. Because you are right, I do not want you here. This is my home and I intend it to stay so.'

She caught her breath at the bluntness of his words, at the calm, arrogant manner in which they were said, and she was helplessly aware that she had invited them upon herself. Forcing herself to speak calmly, she slowly answered him. 'At least we know where we stand. But if I choose not to sell to you, what will you do?'

He shrugged. 'There is nothing I can do. I am no law-breaker.'

'Of course not. It isn''t breaking the law to befriend a wealthy old man and make sure he depends on you, is it?' she lashed out. She heard his indrawn breath and knew instinctively that she had gone too far—but she had to go on. 'So that when he dies——' and then she stopped. The atmosphere was so tense that she felt stifled, and for the first time, physically frightened of what this unpredictable man might do. They were alone—and his face, shadowy though it was, held the tightness of controlled anger.

'Yes?'

'Nothing—I——' she backed slightly away from him.

'Oh, but yes, there is something. So that when he dies I will be sure to have his money—and his *château* —is that how you were going to say it? And are you frightened of me now, so that you dare not?'

Casey looked around them. Bare corridor stretching both ways, and no sounds, only silence filling the air. 'Tell me,' he said, and caught her arm. 'Finish what you started.'

'Let me go! You're hurting me——'

'You are frightened. You think I will hit you? I do not strike women——'

'Then please—you're bruising my arms——'

'I will release you when you finish what you began,' he said harshly.

'All right—yes.' She could always scream for Jack. But would he hear? 'It's happened before——'

'And that is what you think now? You know nothing. Do you hear me? Nothing.' He released her, pushing her away slightly, and she stood there rubbing her arms, unable to move away. Igor looked down at her, eyes smouldering with a controlled kind of temper that struck her as forcibly as a blow. 'You dare to say things when you, who are his flesh and blood, never came near him in the last years of his life? It is

35

you who should be ashamed, not I.'

'He wouldn't let us—he didn't want anyone. I wrote to him—I would have come——'

'You can say that now. Now that it is too late. Then why did you not?'

'Because——' Casey's mind was numbed with the shock and force of his words. It was important that she made things clear—but she sensed that he wouldn't believe anything she said. The antagonism was mutual. 'Because after he quarrelled with my father, several years ago, he cut off all contact with us—and my father died, I wrote to tell him, but he never answered——'

'He was nearly blind—but too stubborn to admit it. Did you not know that? No—you wouldn't—but I knew. He wanted no one to know. You will find a box-ful of letters here, mostly unopened. I helped him, because once, years ago, he had been good to me when I needed help, and I never forget a debt.' He lifted his head proudly, the strong chin jutting, implacable, relentless. 'But for those things you care nothing. Why should you? You were living your busy life, holiday-ing all over the world—oh yes, Miss Cantrell, I have seen your photo in magazines, with your father—"Casey Cantrell, daughter of the wealthy industrialist Mark Cantrell, seen aboard the yacht of Greek ship-ping millionaire Stavros Paxinopoulos where they are holidaying off the Greek Isles"—he mimicked the headlines with a deadly accuracy, for all his accent. 'Oh yes, you have been busy too——'

'You've said enough!'

'But I have scarcely begun. And one way or another, you will listen to me——'

'I won't, I've had enough,' she snapped. 'I don't have to explain myself to you at all.'

'Of course not. Any more than I have to you. But you have listened already. That is a start. People like you are the greedy ones—always wanting more—never happy——'

She hit him again, only harder, and he grabbed hold of her, swung her into the bedroom, and slammed the door shut with his foot. Then with a savageness she had never before known, he kissed her, holding her so tightly she could scarcely breathe. Still holding her in a grip she was completely helpless to resist, he said in her ear: 'How do you like *that*?'

Struggling, her voice muffled with shock, Casey gasped: 'Let me go! You're mad!' She managed to kick his shin—but he appeared not to notice.

'When a woman hits me, I do not hit back. And you have struck me twice. So——' he bent his head, forcing hers back, his mouth seeking hers with an angry intensity. The second kiss was more savage, more violent than the first had been, and Casey felt her legs going weak. Visions of being raped swam into her mind, hazily. She had no strength to fight him, none even to shout.

Then he let her go, and she fell on top of the bed. Igor stood looking down at her. 'Do not hit me again,' he said harshly. 'For you know now what will happen.'

She pulled herself to her feet, holding on to the bed end for support. 'I hate you,' she gasped. 'I hate you!'

'Possibly you do. Do you think I care? I am going now to tend to my garden. That is work—something you have possibly never known——'

'Get out! When I tell Jack——'

He paused on his way to the door. Paused and turned slowly, and looked at her. 'Yes? What will he do?'

'He'll——' she looked at him, saw the incredible toughness that was inherent in him, and knew with a sick inner feeling that he possibly had the strength of two men. A corner of Igor's mouth twitched.

'He will not do anything, because you know better than to tell him.' He paused. 'I do not fight—ever. Do you not know why?' he added softly. She knew. She knew only too well. He nodded, as if seeing the knowledge in her eyes.

'Yes, I can see you do.' He held up his right hand, slowly straightening the fingers of it. 'I have never needed to fight, except purely to defend myself from attack by others—and that has not happened often. Only once, in fact, when I was working on a ship that had docked in Marseilles. Three men came for me one night in a dark alleyway as I left the ship alone——'

'I don't want to hear,' she said dully.

'But I will tell you anyway. They were the kind of people who lie in wait for sailors going off ships—because sailors usually have money to spend. There were three of them, and one of me.' He paused. 'I did not like that. I became angry——'

'Go away,' she said in desperation. 'I don't want to——'

'Then they all had to go to hospital for several days. After which they went to prison.' He held the door. 'So I think it better you do not tell your fiancé.' He paused. 'I do not like unpleasantness.'

The door closed softly behind him. Casey, completely shattered, sat down on the bed. His last words echoed mockingly in her ears. She put her face in her hands, unable to think clearly, everything jumbled up into a nightmarish kaleidoscope of events so confusing that she could not move for several minutes. Then, shakenly, she stood up and went over to open her suitcase.

The scene returned to her in dreams that night so forcefully that she awoke and lay in bed wide-eyed, going over what had happened. Strangely enough, Igor's violence towards her was not uppermost. It was his words when he had told her about herself that came to her most strongly. For the first time in her cushioned existence, she had been forced to see herself through another's eyes. And she hadn't liked what she had seen. She had never questioned her life style before, she had accepted it, enjoyed it, been happy—and now, because of the Russian's harsh assessment, she realised, in an odd way, just how shallow it had all been. Holidays, parties, travelling everywhere in style —she had known nothing else. It was as if he had opened the window on another world. She lay there, eyes open, looking at the ceiling, and saw again his face as they had had their stormy encounter only hours previously. And now at last she knew fully why he didn't want her there.

It was no use. She had to go to the bathroom. It was only three doors away—but where would the dogs be? She lay pondering the subject for a few minutes, and the more she thought about it the more wide awake she became. Very quietly, she got out of bed and crept to the door. Holding the handle tightly to prevent any squeaks, she turned it a fraction of an inch at a time, hardly daring to breathe. So far, so good. Not a creak, not a sound. The door open, she peeped out. A dim light burned at the end of the empty corridor, and she let out her breath and tiptoed along as silently as a ghost, reached the bathroom, opened the door and went inside, closing it firmly after her. 'Phew!' She looked round for the light switch, found it, and gave a beautifully relieved sigh.

A minute or so later she cautiously opened the door again—and a silent black shadow lying outside gave a deep-throated growl. 'Oh, God!' she exclaimed, and shut the door quickly. She stood behind it, her heart going like a hammer, breathing fast as she thought about the situation. Looking round her wasn't much help. All that the room held was that vast, ocean-like bath—in which she eventually had managed a luke-warm wash—a toilet and a wash basin. No juicy bones, with which to bribe a guard dog, were in evidence. She swallowed hard. There was not even a carpet on the floor. The alternative of a few hours' sleep in a cold bath or on even colder tiles was not appealing. Very, very cautiously, she opened the door an inch, and the warning sound came again. It was a polite growl, but one which left her in no doubt that she was considered an intruder and had better stay where she was if she knew what was good for her. Casey knew what was good for her—and it didn't include waiting until daylight in a large bathroom. Then the idea came. Make the dog—or dogs—bark. Someone, probably Boris, would surely hear and investigate. But it needed care. They were probably strong enough to burst the door open, and for Boris to arrive and find her mangled body lying on the floor would prove not only a shock for him but for Casey herself. 'Hmmm,' she thought about that for a few moments. Then she locked the door, knelt down, and whispered: 'Woof-woof!'

There was an interested whine, a snuffling sound, and a cold nose nearly touched hers under the door. Casey backed away hastily. Perhaps the dogs had a sense of humour. She didn't intend to put it to the test. What would make them *bark*? There seemed only one thing for it—noise. Lots of it—which might also serve the double purpose of waking Boris. She went over to the window, opened it, then slammed it shut again, at the same time shouting: 'Help, help!'

The next second everything erupted. The dogs began barking furiously, and Casey went to the door and started banging on it as loudly as she could. She could hardly stand the noise herself. Then an angry voice shouted something in Russian, and the next moment there came a violent hammering on the door.

Casey opened it to see Igor's face staring at her, a dog each side of him. He took one look at her, turned and spoke gently to the dogs, then back to her.

'What are you doing? Are you mad?' he demanded.

'I couldn't get out,' she said, keeping her eyes firmly fixed on his face. He wore a short black towelling robe, and if he had anything on underneath it she would be surprised—and had no intention of finding out. 'I'm sorry. I came to the bathroom and when I tried to come out, one of the dogs was waiting outside——' she was babbling, but she couldn't help it. The flimsy cotton nightie she wore did nothing for her dignity, nor did the whole situation.

'I warned you——'

'I know. But I woke up and—and——' she swallowed. 'Oh! I'm not standing here explaining to *you* —heavens, it's not a crime to want to go to the bathroom in the middle of the night, is it?' she glared at him helplessly.

'We will work something out in the morning,' he answered. 'Come—to your room.' He spoke again to the two dogs, and they padded silently away down the corridor. Reaching behind Casey, Igor switched off the light and took her arm. It was a gesture oddly surprising, coming from *him*, and she stiffened. Then, as he ushered her along, she relaxed slightly. It meant nothing, merely his haste to despatch her back to her room. Outside the door he stopped.

'My room is next to this one,' he said. She saw the light streaming from it, cutting a swathe across the passage. 'If you need anything else during the night, I suggest you knock on my wall first.'

She said the first thing that came into her head. 'You must be joking!' She regretted it, of course, an instant later, but it was too late then. He looked her slowly up and down, and then smiled.

'Joking? I must be—after what happened this evening.' He nodded. She drew in her breath sharply, stung by the dismissive nature of his glance.

'Thank you for telling me where your room is— I'll make sure I keep my door locked in future,' she retorted.

About to walk away from her, he paused, and turned. 'You have no need to, I assure you. I could have no reason for wishing to enter your room—ever.'

She stared at his retreating back; the door closed, the light was cut off. Then silence. Casey went into her own room and closed the door. He was absolutely detestable! She didn't think she had ever disliked anyone so much before. But worse, far worse, was the feeling of utter helplessness. It was as if he would always manage to have the last word. She climbed into bed, feeling vaguely disturbed and totally confused. For she had never met anyone to whom she reacted so strongly, and that feeling was infinitely more unsettling.

Things always assume a different look by daylight,

and so it proved. Casey and Jack ate an excellent French breakfast with Boris in the kitchen, and bright sunlight streamed through the windows. Jack glanced briefly at her as they sat down at the table. 'Didn't you sleep well?' he asked. 'You look tired.'

'I'm fine, thanks,' she answered briefly. She had not mentioned the scene before her bath to him, and had no intention of telling him about the second nocturnal encounter—and he looked disgustingly cheerful and wide awake, which did nothing to improve Casey's humour.

Boris put a plateful of hot flaky croissants on the table. 'Please eat,' he said. 'Mr Borodinov asks you to excuse him, he is working outside, but will show you around when you have breakfasted.' She hadn't expected him to eat with them, so that came as no surprise to Casey, but Jack lifted a cynical eyebrow and gave her an 'I told you so' glance, which she ignored. She was still feeling out of sorts—as well as tired, due to the fact that she had slept badly after her visit to the bathroom. She wanted nothing so much as to lie down again and sleep.

'Are you sure you're all right?' asked Jack solicitously.

'Yes. Sure.' She spread apricot jam on a croissant and bit into it, and a while later, when they had finished the meal with hot coffee, she began to feel better. She had always been able to think over any problems, and sort them out within herself—and there was no way she could even begin to tell Jack anything of what had happened, without him causing a major scene, and in any case, she reflected, as they left the kitchen, I don't know what's wrong myself. Except that Igor Borodinov is possibly the most awkward man living and has the ability to make me feel uneasy just by looking at me—and I couldn't tell anyone, least of all Jack, that.

Boris led them into the front hall. 'Shall we go outside and find him?' he said.

Sure, why not? thought Casey. He's probably picking some deadly nightshade—or poison mushrooms—to serve us at dinner. He'll be delighted to see us. The thought restored, in part, her good humour and she merely said: 'Of course. I'd like to see the gardens anyway.'

Jack took her arm as they went down the steps, which gave her an unfortunate reminder of Igor, and caused her to jerk her arm away and say: 'I can manage, thanks.'

Jack glanced at her. 'A bit snappy, aren't you?' Boris had gone on ahead of them, cutting across the grass in the direction of the greenhouses, so that whatever they said would be unheard.

'Am I? Sorry.' She gave him a smile. One foe was enough. More than enough, considering who it was. Jack was far easier to deal with, but she could do without him sulking—and that he was perfectly capable of, as she well knew. 'I didn't actually sleep very well, but I didn't want to say so in front of Boris. *He's* doing his best to look after us.' The accent of the 'he' was not lost on Jack, who nodded thoughtfully.

'Yes, true. The other one, your co-owner, is hardly the most amiable soul around, is he?'

'No.' But she didn't want to talk about Igor. 'Oh, look—are those olive trees?' she exclaimed, as if it were very important.

Jack shrugged. 'Could be. A bit twisted and old, aren't they?'

She laughed. 'They're supposed to be!'

'Hmmm—oh, oh, there's lover boy. But who the hell's he talking to?'

She looked. Boris had reached Igor, who was digging away, but not alone. Two children stood watching him, and all four were apparently engrossed in conversation. They were at the side of the greenhouse, and one child—a girl—carried a basket. She was dressed in a plain blue shift dress, and was barefoot. Her companion, a boy of perhaps eight or nine, stood by her side. He too was plainly clad in blue shorts. Boris turned to Casey and Jack, and Igor at last looked at them.

Curious now, Casey walked nearer, leaving Jack to follow her. 'I shall not be long,' said Igor, digging his spade in the earth and resting his hand on the handle. 'Show them the greenhouses, Boris.'

'Of course.' But Casey remained where she was as Jack obediently followed the Russian manservant. Her curiosity overcame her dislike.

'Who are these?' she said.

Igor glanced coolly at her. 'My friends.' He said something to them in French—either not knowing or not caring if Casey understood.

'This lady has come to see the *château*,' he said. 'It

46

is half hers.' They both turned and looked solemnly at her. Casey smiled and in her most immaculate French, said:

'Yes, I have, and I think it's very beautiful. Do you live near here?'

The girl answered, taking hold of her brother's hand as she spoke.

'We live down there,' and she nodded towards a thick belt of trees. 'M'sieur Igor gives us many vegetables—and in return we help him with his gardens.'

'I'm sure you do.' Casey looked at the boy, who had regarded her unwinkingly and silently ever since she had arrived.

There was a brief silence, then Igor answered—in English: 'He does not speak.'

Casey's eyes widened in shock. 'Oh, you mean he's a mute?' A wave of pity washed over her.

'No. He simply does not choose to. I'll tell you why later.' He turned to the children and spoke to them in French. 'I'm going indoors now. You must go home to your mother—but you may come back later. Come, I will give you some vegetables I picked for you earlier.'

He held out his hand and the girl took it, leaving her brother to follow. She watched them go towards the second greenhouse, the little girl looking up trustingly at Igor, and chattering away. They made an odd but strangely moving picture, the big man and the two small children. He laughed at something she said, and was a world away from the hostile aggressor of the previous night. He spoke softly to them—and he looked around, as if he knew that Casey watched him —and his face had changed too. He was relaxed, and he possessed that quality of gentleness that is supposed to be in every truly strong man—and Casey felt a stirring within her, but understood it not at all. Then she followed them, because she could not do otherwise. They stood just inside the steaming hot greenhouse, with water sprays nourishing the long plant-filled soil beds, then Igor filled the girl's basket with ripe firm tomatoes and lettuces and onions until it was crammed full. Casey was unobserved. He had not looked round again. She watched from outside the doorway, saw him reach in his pocket and take out some coins which he gave to the boy, and they vanished instantly into the boy's pocket.

'Off you go,' he said. 'Straight home.'

She heard the little girl whisper something, saw Igor bend his head to hear—then he burst out laughing. And as he did so, he looked round and saw Casey. '*Non!*' he said. '*Absolument non!*' And Casey knew in that instant that the question had concerned her.

The little girl came out holding her brother's hand again, and looked at Casey. '*Au revoir, mademoiselle,*' she said.

'*Au revoir.*' She watched them go. She could see Jack and Boris faintly through the whitewashed glass of the other greenhouse. 'Why doesn't the boy talk?' she asked Igor.

'Emil? Nobody knows—except that he nearly drowned two years ago, and when he was pulled out of the water he was unconscious.' He shrugged. 'He's not said a word since. There's no medical reason—or none that anyone can discover. He hears, and he listens, but he won't answer you.'

'How sad.'

'There are worse things in life. He is happy enough.' She looked sharply at him. He had changed again. Yet she knew instinctively that his behaviour towards the children had not been an act. Therefore, and perhaps logically, the only reason for his cynical reply was that he preferred not to discuss the children with Casey. She could hardly blame him.

She changed the subject before he could. 'We'd like to see round the *château*, if it's convenient.'

He gave her a cool hard glance. 'It isn't—but I will show you.'

She felt her mouth tighten. Jack and Boris were still talking, well out of earshot. 'I've got a nice bruise on my arm—thanks to you.' She rolled up the short sleeve of her yellow blouse. Igor looked at her without expression.

'You should not try and fight me.'

'Is that all you can say?'

'For now—yes.'

'You're a bully!'

'I think not. It is not my fault that you bruise easily. Be thankful that it isn't on your face, or your fiancé might have something to say.' He smiled, without humour. 'You did not tell him, of course?'

'Did you imagine I would, so you'd have an excuse to

49

beat him up?' She smiled. 'I'm not so stupid.'

'Perhaps you are learning,' he answered.

'Learning what? I don't need you to teach me anything,' she retorted swiftly.

'Somebody should.' The brief truce that had existed while the children were present had vanished. The air around them crackled with the mutual tension—but the setting was different from before. Here was no lonely shadowy corridor, but sunshine, heat and light. But it had not changed. The mutual antagonism was as potent as ever—and both were startlingly aware of it, Igor particularly. His face was an implacable mask of sheer strength. 'You will learn, before you leave here, exactly who you are.'

'I already know.'

'Do you? I wonder.' He smiled.

'And if I don't choose to leave?' she demanded.

He raised a thick eyebrow. 'Ah, I see. You have decided to stay, then?' It was not the answer she had expected.

'I might do.'

'With Jack—your fiancé?'

'I don't know. That's none of your business.'

'Perhaps not, but he wants you to sell—I do not think he would be happy here, any more than you would. Nor do I think he would go away and leave you here with me.' That was a highly accurate guess—but nothing more, unless of course Igor had been listening at the door, and she wouldn't put that past him.

'I do what I want,' she snapped, childishly she knew,

50

but she couldn't think of anything better to say.

'I'm quite sure that you do, and that you always have.' He held up his hands, calloused and black with the rich earth. 'But you have never worked. All has been easy for you.'

'I'm capable.' She lifted her chin defiantly. 'Nothing's impossible.'

'Nothing? Then how would you like to do some gardening—with me, later today?' The brown eyes met hers in a hard challenge.

She had fallen beautifully into the trap, and they both knew it. She had only to say no ... 'All right,' said Casey. 'I will. I'll show you.'

CHAPTER FOUR

THE only trouble was—how did she tell Jack? As they walked back to the *château*, he glanced curiously at her, then at Igor walking ahead with Boris. 'What the hell goes on with you two?' he asked, his mouth tight with disapproval. 'For someone you don't like, you seem to have some very chummy conversations.'

Chummy, thought Casey, is hardly the word I would use. 'He was implying that I didn't know what work was—which annoyed me—and then he more or less challenged me to do some gardening. He expected me to refuse, of course.'

'Which you did?'

'Well, no, actually. I said yes.'

'Good grief! You can count me out. I've got plans to finish.'

'Yes, I thought you'd say that.'

Jack ignored that remark. 'Just watch him, that's all. I wouldn't trust him further than I could throw him.'

'Which wouldn't be very far,' she murmured.

'What's that supposed to mean?' He stopped walking and stared at her. 'I don't know what's got into you since we arrived. You're very edgy.'

Casey bit her lip. 'I'm sorry, Jack—I'm tired, that's all.'

'Huh! And gardening won't improve the situation.'

'I know. You don't need to rub it in,' she sighed.

'You can always say you've changed your mind. You're here for a holiday, not to work.'

'As he's implied—none too subtly—that my life is one long holiday already, I'm sure he wouldn't be in the slightest bit surprised.'

'Well, let's face it, it is, isn't it? I mean, you've never had to work for a living, have you?'

They were still standing facing each other, and Casey became aware simultaneously of two things. One—Igor had stopped and was waiting in the doorway watching them, and two—Jack, the man she loved, the man who told her frequently that he could not live without her, was making a very creditable effort to start a quarrel. It had happened before, of course. She was usually able to laugh things off. But this last remark of his, for some reason, stung her.

'Would you like me to get a job when we get back to London?' she asked very quietly.

'What at?' he asked bluntly. 'Secretary? You can't type——'

'I could learn,' she retorted.

'Oh, sure you could. After a while.' He shrugged. 'Why worry anyway? When we're married you won't need to. It strikes me you're letting that big oaf get under your skin——'

'It looks like he's getting under yours too,' she answered.

'Yes—okay, if you want to know, he does. I don't like him——'

53

'That's obvious.' Her eyes sparkled with anger. Let *him* watch if he wanted. She didn't care.

'And whose side are you on anyway?' Jack demanded. 'You don't like him either—or do you?'

Casey began to walk away from him and he caught her wrist.

'Let me go, you fool! He's watching us——'

'Let him. Do you?'

'Like him? Of course not. I'm going in.' She jerked her hand free and walked on, and after a moment's hesitation, Jack followed. She ran up the steps to see Igor standing in the doorway.

'Ready?' he asked quietly. Nothing showed. His face was bland and quite devoid of the expression she had expected.

'Yes.'

'Then I will show you around the *château*.' He waited politely for Jack, turned, and opened the inner door, gesturing for Casey to go through first. She went in. She felt unhappy and confused.

It was nearly two hours later that they finished their grand tour. The Château Fleuron was truly vast, with so many rooms that she lost count after the first twenty or so. It was structurally sound, but so many of the rooms were unfurnished and cold, yet withal there was a beauty about the place, despite the antique plumbing and the shabby furniture which had been in for years.

When they had seen everywhere, and had reached

the final room high in a turret, Casey looked out of the window, and she could see for miles. Distantly was the sea, still and calm in the morning sun. Between the *château* and the sea were rich trees and woodland and fields, with the occasional glimpse of a pantiled roof. She leaned on the windowsill, uncaring of the two impatient men waiting silently by the door.

Jack coughed. 'Ahem—ready, Casey?'

She answered without turning round: 'In a minute. You go if you want. I'll find my way down—I'm enjoying the view.' She wanted to be left alone to think, and she couldn't do it with those two standing there. She wished they would both go. She could almost feel Jack's indecision. If he left, would Igor leave too? She turned.

'I'm all right—I won't get lost.' This with a brief glance at the Russian.

Jack shrugged. 'I want to get on with those plans—I'll be in my room.'

'Yes. I won't be long myself.' She turned back. Then she heard footsteps going down the corridor—two pairs of footsteps. She sighed, drew up a chair—the only item of furniture in the room, a hard wooden high-backed chair, and sat on it, leaning her elbows on the window ledge. Then she began to think. She was impressed by what she had seen, had even felt, occasionally, the pleasure of possession. It was not hers alone, but nevertheless she had a half of it, and there was a certain satisfaction in walking through the tall high-ceilinged rooms, some with faded tapestries from bygone years lining the walls, others with stained glass windows that allowed in coloured lights in intricate designs, and possessed a rare quality of beauty. And one strange and disturbing fact had emerged as they had gone on their journey. Igor belonged there. In a way she could not begin to explain, even to herself, he was part of it. He had been different again as he showed them each part of the enormous *château*. Tall and proud—not arrogant—he had led them through the rooms, and every word he spoke told of the love he had for the place.

Casey put her chin in her hand. He belongs here, and I don't, she thought. He's like some medieval knight—which was an absurd thought to have, but it was there, and it would not go away. Then she discovered, to her horror, that she was crying. The tears trickled down her cheeks and plopped on to the stone ledge, and a voice came from the doorway:

'I thought that you were lost again.'

'I was—lost in the view.' She began hastily and furtively rubbing at her cheeks, not daring to look round lest he see. And Igor walked—no, padded—silently across from the door.

'Why are you weeping?' he asked.

She sniffed. 'I—I'm not.' The next moment he put his hand under her chin and turned her to face him. She saw a muscle tighten in his cheeks, and then he released her.

'Why?'

She blinked. 'I—nothing. I can cry if I want to, can't I?'

'Is it because you and Jack have quarrelled?'

She stared at him blankly. She had forgotten all about it.

'Of course not! It's just——' she waved her hand vaguely towards the outside, 'it's so beautiful, that's all.'

'And that makes you sad?'

She stood up. 'Leave me alone, will you? I don't have to answer your questions.' The room was too small for them both. She wanted to be away from him. The less they were alone, the better. 'We should go down now. Where's Jack?'

'In his room working. And you are coming out with me.' It was a statement, not a question.

'Now?'

'Yes. Before the sun is too hot.'

'What are we going to do?'

'You will see. Have you any working clothes?'

Her heart sank. 'I've got a pair of old jeans, yes.'

'Good. They will be better than your dress.' His eyes narrowed, became hard. 'Unless you have changed your mind?'

She looked at him. 'You'd like that, wouldn't you? I can just see your face if I said I wasn't going to bother——'

'But you will not. It is a matter of pride now. Is that why you argued with Jack? About that?'

Casey stared stonily at him. 'You're very impertinent.'

'Yes, I know. If I wish to know anything, I ask. It is quite simple.'

She took a deep breath. His sheer arrogance swept the ground from beneath her at times. But two could play at that game. And let's see if you like it, she thought. 'How old are you?' she asked.

'Thirty-six.'

'And how long have you lived in France?'

'Sixteen years.'

'Are you married—or do you have a girl-friend?' She paused, then added softly: 'Or both?'

He was beginning to look amused, not annoyed. 'Neither. I have no time for a woman in my life.'

'A pity,' she retorted, trying to shake his apparently magnificent complacency. 'One might make you more human.'

'Like Jack is?' Softly enquiring.

'Leave him out of this!'

'But why? You are asking, and telling me things. Why should I not ask in return?' He shrugged gracefully. 'Have you made him more human, as you put it?'

'I like to think so.'

'Then what was he like before, I wonder?' He smiled. Casey had had enough. She knew she should never have started it anyway. She moved from him and picked up her bag from the back of the chair.

'I'm going down,' she said. 'I'd rather not talk to you—you're quite impossible. I'd rather be working. I'll go and change into my jeans.' She swung the bag strap on to her shoulder and walked towards the door. Igor opened it and she went through and into the corridor, dark after the sunshine of the turret room. He walked beside her, and the passage was so narrow that they were almost touching, which made Casey uncomfortable. He seemed unaware of the fact. At the head of the spiral staircase which led down to the second floor of the *château*, he stopped and said:

'I will go first.'

'Wait.' Casey had suddenly remembered something. 'What was it the little girl whispered to you that made you laugh and answer, "absolutely not?"'

'Marie?' he frowned for a moment, as if trying to remember, then his mouth twitched. 'Ah—*yes*,' and he began to laugh again. Then he shook his head. 'No, it was unimportant.'

'Tell me!'

He looked down at her. 'She asked me if you were my wife,' he answered. 'Now do you see why I found it so funny?' And he turned away and began descending the stairs.

For some reason—probably because it was the only task she had seen him doing—Casey expected Igor to hand her a spade and tell her to start digging by the greenhouses. But when she had changed and met him in the front hall, he led her outside away from the house and towards the thick belt of trees some distance away. When they had nearly reached them, Casey looked at him.

'Where are we going?' she asked him.

He paused in his loping stride. 'You will soon see.'

'But I thought we'd be digging.' She pointed back towards the greenhouses.

'That can wait for today. Come, we will soon be there.' He strode on easily, so that she nearly had to run to keep apace. Into the wood, and it was cool and shady, greenly lit with the sun filtering through the leaves, and Casey wondered if perhaps she shouldn't have changed her mind when she'd had the chance. Deeper and deeper into the trees they went, and she felt completely lost—and not a little apprehensive. It was all very well accepting challenges, but she had no idea where they were going, or what she was letting herself in for—and Jack's remarks came back to perturb her further.

'Look,' she said. 'Wait a moment—I—look, tell me where we're going, please.'

Momentarily his eyes lost their usual hardness. 'Are you frightened of me?'

'Of course not.' She tried to sound amused, but it didn't quite come off. 'But I haven't a clue where we are.'

'Then stay with me. *I* know,' came the hardly reassuring answer, and on he loped. She looked back. Nothing except trees, trees, and more trees. She was already well lost. Perhaps they would just go on walking for ever. She tried to visualise the scene from the tower window, to remember what she could see—but it was no use.

Then suddenly the trees began to thin. Ahead of them lay a clearing, with a tumbledown cottage, and nearby a lake—and paddling on the edges of the lake were several geese. 'Oh!' Casey stopped, and looked. Igor stopped as well, glancing at her in some amusement.

'Wild geese,' he said, as if explaining to a child. 'And very rare in this part of the world. And one of them has a damaged wing and cannot fly, so his companions stay with him and keep him company. Watch.' He felt in his jeans pocket and brought out a squashed plastic bag full of pieces of bread. Then he whistled, and the geese came waddling over, honking madly, scrambling to reach where they stood. One was slower than the rest. Beautifully coloured in iridescent shades of grey and blue, it hovered at the rear of its fellows as if unsure of Casey.

Igor flung most of the bread to the ground, and there was a mad scramble for it. Then, walking soft-footed over to the remaining bird, he began to feed it by hand. Casey stood where she was, watching, knowing it wiser not to move lest she frighten it. Igor was making soft noises as he fed it, and the goose responded, eyes bright, grabbing the morsels of bread greedily from his hand. I don't believe it, she thought. And Jack wouldn't either. Jack would think Igor was mad. He stood up and walked back to where Casey waited, rubbing the crumbs from his hands.

'And now to work,' he said.

She looked around her. 'Here?'

'No. This way.' He began walking at the side of the lake, away from the geese. Casey looked back. The bread had vanished, every last crumb, and the birds were once more paddling in their territory.

'How did it happen?' she asked him.

'I don't know.' He shrugged. 'I found him one day, after I heard Emil——' he stopped.

'Who? Emil? The little boy—but you said he never spoke——'

'This was the lake he nearly drowned in.'

'Oh! You mean—it was you——'

'I pulled him out, yes.' He looked at her. 'Then I carried him to his home. And that is how I came to know the family. They live not far away. We will visit them after, when we are finished.'

There was an incredible amount of information to digest in those few words, and Casey took her time about it. He had saved the boy's life, but not bothered to mention it before. He visited the family—and he looked after an injured wild goose. What next? she wondered rather dazedly. She was soon to find out.

He had not seen fit to mention where they were going, either, or what they would be doing. And it wasn't until they saw a small cottage nearby that he stopped and pointed. 'Emil and Marie live there.' She looked. The house was in sad need of repair, with paint peeling off the shutters, and a generally neglected air. A broken chair leaned drunkenly against the wall, and a line of washing moved slightly in the faintest of breezes. Somewhere a baby cried, and she could see that the door of the cottage was open. Casey experienced an overwhelming feeling of sadness. She looked at Igor.

'Yes,' he said. 'They are very poor.'

'Can't anything be done?'

'Give them money?' He smiled drily. 'Wait until you meet their father, then you will see.' He indicated the neglected patch of garden. 'This is where we are going to work. I have promised that I will make them a vegetable garden so that they can grow their own food. And today we are digging that section up.' She looked at it. It was far worse than she had expected, weed-filled, the ground as hard as stone, baked by the hot sun.

'Yes, I see,' she said.

'And hard work. Come, we will let them know we are here. There are spades here for us—or there were a few days ago.' She didn't understand precisely what he meant then—that comprehension came later.

As they walked towards the house, Marie ran out of the door, followed by her brother, Emil. 'M'sieur Igor,' she shrieked joyfully, 'you have come!' She flung her arms up and Igor bent and swung her upwards.

'Yes, we are here to work. You are going to help us, hey?'

'Maman, he is here, M'sieur Igor is here with the young lady.' A woman appeared at the door, wiping her hands on a tattered apron. She was painfully thin, with long dark hair, and traces of a former beauty in her face.

'Bonjour,' she murmured. Igor shook hands with her, then introduced Casey.

He spoke to her in French. 'We are beginning the garden today, Madame Gallion. The spades are here?'

'Yes. I hid them——' a brief, nervous glance at Casey. 'It was better he did not know. You are very kind, *m'sieur*. Will you take a little wine before you begin? And you, *mademoiselle*?'

'No, thank you,' Igor answered for them both. He spoke gently to the woman, as he had before to the children, who now waited patiently near him. 'We will work for an hour or so and then return later.' A baby cried from within the house, and the woman disappeared, to return a moment later carrying a smaller version of Marie, a girl about one year old, dressed in a vest. She rocked the baby as she gave instructions to Marie and Emil, who then darted away towards a ramshackle shed. They came back dragging two large spades, which Igor took from them and turned to Casey.

'This one is yours,' he told her. 'Are you ready?'

'Yes.' She was beginning to feel completely dazed with all that had happened, and was happening. Nothing had prepared her for this, and she had never before seen such abject poverty close to. She felt helpless in the face of it, torn with a deep pity that was so overwhelming it almost made her feel ill. And what kind of man was Igor? Not completely the rough aggressive man she had thought. There was this unexpected side to him that confused her. She began to look forward to the undoubtedly hard task ahead. At least it would stop her thinking.

And it was hard. After fifteen minutes of sheer determined digging, with little to show for it, she was exhausted. The two children had been set the work of pulling up weeds from the dry ground, and Igor dug silently away, yards from her, and already the black rich soil underneath was being revealed. Casey watched him briefly as she paused to take a few deep breaths, and could not help but admire his method, despite her personal feelings. His pace was steady and sure, and he was seemingly untired and untiring. Turning away, knowing her own efforts were puny in comparison, Casey began digging again.

Time passed, the sun rose higher, and they worked in silence. She was bathed in perspiration, and her hands were slippery on the spade, and every muscle in her body cried out for her to stop—but she went on. And when, aeons afterwards, she heard the unbelievable words: 'We'll stop now,' she could scarcely appreciate them.

Igor was watching her. She dragged her spade up out of the soil and stared dizzily at him. 'Finish?' she croaked. She was trying hard not to sway.

'Yes. It is lunchtime—past. Boris and Jack will wonder where we are.' He turned and walked away. 'Wait there a moment.' Marie stood up and flung a handful of weeds away and smiled shyly at Casey. Her brother still knelt, intent on his weeding. Igor had vanished into the cottage, and she heard faint voices talking, then he came out, and over to where Casey waited.

'Let's go,' he said. The anger on his face startled her.

'What——' she began.

'Wait. Do not talk.' She was frightened. Had she done something? He shouted goodbye to the children and then strode away towards the trees. Bewildered, oddly apprehensive, Casey followed him. Had she not worked hard enough? But she had done her best. Surely he didn't expect miracles? She would come again. She had to, although she could not have explained why. His anger was the more frightening because she didn't know the reason for it. And when they were well in the trees, and it was cool and shadowy, and she had her breath back, she said:

'What have I done?' They might as well have it out now as later.

He stopped and looked at her. 'You? What have *you* done?'

'You're angry. Tell me why.'

He looked away. It was worse than she feared. Was he too angry to speak? It was beginning to seem like a living nightmare. Then he turned to her.

'I am not angry with you,' he said.

'Oh!' The relief was almost overwhelming. 'Then —not their *mother*?' That was even more incredible.

'No.' He added a word that was probably in Russian, and most undoubtedly an expletive, so brief and violent was it, then he looked at Casey. 'Her husband. The only man I could kill without feeling the slightest remorse.' The violence of his words was shocking.

'Oh—no!' She stared at him helplessly, seeing the burning anger in his eyes.

'If I gave them money, he would take it and drink

himself stupid—and then he would beat them. As he does frequently.' His eyes narrowed. 'He beats the children——'

'But can't you do anything about it? Tell the police——'

'She is frightened of him, too frightened to complain. She has nowhere to go—and he would find her if she did leave. He is a sick man, and a very bad one——'

'But you can't—you can't just let it go like that, Igor——' she clutched his arm in desperation, 'you must do something to help them.'

'I have tried. He can be normal, sometimes. Then I can talk to him, although that is not easy. He suspects everyone who tries to help. I am doing what I can, and that is all anyone can do.'

'No, it isn't. There must be more.' She looked at him. 'At the back of the *château*—those outbuildings that were once stables—couldn't they be converted into a home for Madame Gallion and the children?'

The tight anger had left his face. He was calmer. 'Why are you concerned? It is nothing to do with you?'

'It is now. *You* took me there, remember?'

'To teach you what work was—yes, I remember.' He smiled. 'And now you surprise me.'

'Why? Did you think that because I was rich and idle I had no feelings?' she demanded. It was now on a personal level. They were getting back to normal.

He nodded. 'Possibly.'

'Which just proves how wrong you are,' she retorted smartly. She glared at him. 'And that makes us even. I thought you were an unfeeling brute.'

'*Touché.*' The anger had completely vanished. 'Perhaps I am—in many things of life. But not where helpless creatures are concerned.'

Then he mustn't think *I'm* a helpless creature, she thought—but she forbore to say it. For the moment a fragile truce existed. Not only would it not do any good to spoil it, but Casey wanted desperately to help the Gallion family. She did not know them, had only met children and mother briefly, but her deepest feelings were stirred—and she had an extremely determined nature. 'Well,' she said, 'are we going to look at those buildings or not?'

'Now?'

'Yes. Now. Before you forget why you were angry. While it is still fresh in your mind—and why were you so angry anyway? Was he in the house?'

'Yes.' He began walking again towards home. 'He was sobering up—and had just got out of bed when I went in. He resents me giving them food—he will eat it—but he possesses that strange twisted pride that makes him hate the giver. And he——' Igor paused and looked at Casey. 'And he thinks that any man who goes near the house must be after his wife.' His mouth tightened. 'His language can be vile. It was best I left.'

'And you *let* him insult you?' She shook her head, disbelieving. 'I wouldn't have thought——' She stopped. She was treading on thin ice. She saw his crooked grin.

'Yes,' he answered. 'You cannot imagine that, can you? But think—if I had hit him—and the temptation is great, have no doubt about that—what would he do after I had gone?'

She knew, with a sick feeling. 'Oh.'

'And what effect would it have on the children to see someone giving their father a beating? No, I do the only thing possible. I walk out. But one day, when he is alone——' he paused, to let out his breath. 'Come, hurry. Boris will be saying to Jack that we are lost— and what will your fiancé think then, hey?'

Casey knew what her fiancé would think, without Igor telling her.

'I'm still going to look after lunch,' she said. 'Will you come with me?'

He shrugged, scarcely slowing his walk to let her catch up. 'Perhaps. You make up your mind quickly, do you not?'

'Yes, when I need to.' She had a pain in her side. 'Please slow down, I have a stitch.'

He slowed imperceptibly. 'Stitch? What is that?'

She rubbed her waist at the right side. 'You know, a pain from hurrying—and after the gardening.'

'And how did you like that?'

'It was rough work.' She looked at him. Was it possible that his face wasn't quite as hard as usual? 'But I managed, didn't I?'

'Not badly.'

'Oh, please,' she murmured, still rubbing her side, 'don't overdo the praise. You can't imagine how it goes to my head.'

He began to laugh. He was so different, she suddenly thought. It was a laugh of genuine amusement, and his face changed, laughter lines creasing at the sides of his eyes, white strong teeth gleaming. 'Ah yes, I like that,' he said. 'Sometimes—perhaps—you English can be funny.'

'We try—ouch!' she doubled up in sudden pain, stopped walking, and leaned against a tree. Igor turned towards her, moved nearer, and she gasped: 'No, leave me. It'll pass.' Her arm pressed against her side, she had a sudden wave of pain, and nauseated, bit her lip.

'Casey, what is it?' There was anxiety on his face. He was actually *concerned*.

She managed to straighten up. 'It's gone now. I'm sorry. It was nothing—I must have pulled a muscle or something.' Some of her spirit returned. 'Don't worry, I won't blame you. I did volunteer to work, after all.' She could breathe again. She could even look calmly at him. But she didn't know how white her face was.

He suddenly put his hand to her waist. 'Is that where it hurts?'

'Yes.' She wished he would not touch her. His hand was warm and strong—but gentle. 'Please—I——'

'Just *there*?'

She winced. 'Oh—yes. What are you doing?'

'It is a nerve. You have trapped a nerve. Sometimes it happens when you are not used to exertion. I will rub it—see.' Very gently he massaged the area round her waist, and Casey, with a sudden awareness and shock, wondered if she didn't prefer the agony of before—because this was infinitely more disturbing. In fact . . .

'Look,' she whispered, 'I'm all right——' but she wasn't. She was far from all right. All her senses a-flame, she was suddenly, frighteningly aware of him as a man—far more so than when he had so violently kissed her—because now he was being infinitely tender, and it was more confusing, and she wanted him to stop. To stop right now.

'Just relax.' It was as though he knew. 'If you go and lie down on your bed I can cure it for you.' She wanted to laugh, but she couldn't. She closed her eyes. The next moment she was in his arms.

CHAPTER FIVE

THAT at least brought Casey to her senses. She tried to push him away.

'I thought you were going to faint,' Igor said, as he released her. 'Are you all right?'

'No—yes—I don't know,' she croaked, totally confused. She was, for the moment, trying desperately to picture Jack's face, to restore her sanity. Because he was the man she loved, and this—this Russian brute was merely someone who had happened to be there. She cleared her throat. 'Er—the pain's gone now,' she managed. She stood upright. It had too. 'That's better.'

'Then you are sure?'

'Quite sure.'

'I think, perhaps, no more digging for you today,' he said quietly. 'Can you walk? We are late.'

'Yes, I'm fine.' They set off again, a shade more slowly. 'If you—we—decide to let the Gallions move in at the *château*,' she said. 'We won't need to do any more digging anyway, will we?'

'You think it is as simple as that? We decide? That is all? Have you considered what Madame Gallion might feel? It is her home, after all——'

'But you said——' she felt bewildered, 'you said he beat them. And she looks very unhappy. Surely she'd jump at the chance to get away.'

'I do not understand the ways of a woman's mind, Casey. I once asked her that—if she would leave if she had the opportunity, and she looked at me blankly, then said: "But he is my husband, *m'sieur*."'

'That's logical, I suppose,' she admitted. 'He is. Would it help if I talked to her?'

'You can try. He will be out when we return. Perhaps then you can talk. He will be away down to the *auberge* in the village, drinking himself senseless. But I warn you—take care.'

'You don't think I'm going to try and scare her, do you?' she retorted. It was far better when they were on sparring terms again. At least she knew where she was with him. But not when he was so gentle .... She hastily put certain thoughts from her mind. 'I shall —just talk, that's all. I can't plan ahead what I am going to say. I shall wait and see.'

They could see the *château* ahead of them now that they had left the trees behind, and the stone walls glittered in the sun. Casey looked briefly at Igor. It's ours, she thought. We share that place, we two strangers who dislike each other, and yet—and Igor turned and caught her expression.

'What are you thinking?' he asked.

'Nothing much,' she answered. 'Except how beautiful the *château* is.' We have that link, she thought. The link of sharing a place, and it is a strange one, for even though there is this mutual distrust, yet sometimes I feel as if we were meant to meet. It was such an odd idea to have that she shivered, suddenly cold, despite the sun. Crossing the grass, near the green-houses now. Jack will be waiting, she thought. Good old Jack, I'm glad I came with him. I do love him— and he soon gets things in perspective, especially about Igor. Then Igor spoke:

'You know that it is nearly three o'clock? Jack will not be very happy, I think.'

She looked sharply at him. Was he a mind-reader? 'He'll understand when I tell him,' she answered blithely. And added inwardly, and very silently—I hope.

'Yes.' That was all he said. It was a long-drawn-out, even a questioning, yes. It spoke volumes. And the moment was ripe, Casey decided, to correct a certain mistaken opinion of Igor's.

'I know you don't like my fiancé,' she said, emphas-ising with great subtlety those last two words, 'but he's very nice really, and it's very kind of him to take time off work and come here with me, because he's an ex-ceedingly busy architect.'

'Yes, of course.' Three more volumes of words. Casey felt her scalp prickle.

'There's no need to say it like *that*!' she burst out, exasperated.

'How would you like me to say it?' he answered, amused. 'I am trying to be nice to you—or did you not notice?'

'Oh!' She stared at him. He was the most utterly maddening man! 'Then I suggest you don't try—it— it doesn't become you!' She had done it again. What on earth's up with me? she thought. I can't seem to help myself . . .

'So, I will become nasty, and then you will be happy, yes?'

'No—oh!' She felt like stamping her foot, which would not only have been childish, but ridiculous. 'Let's just try and be civilised, shall we?'

'We can try. The only trouble is, can you?'

'What do you mean?' They had reached the front entrance, and at the top of the steps, in the cool porch, she stopped and looked at him.

'You are not an easy person to get on with——' he began.

'Me! *Me?*' she squeaked. 'I'm very easy-going—all my friends will tell you——'

'But I am not one of your friends. I am the Russian stranger with whom you unwillingly share this *château*—and whom you suspect of all kinds of base things, like for example becoming friendly with a sick old man that I might inherit his wealth——' he spoke quietly, but the force of his words provided far greater emphasis than if he had shouted.

'I——' she began feebly, 'I might have been mistaken——'

'But you thought it—and your fiancé also thinks it, does he not? And some things I do not forget——'

'Well, you told me that Jack wasn't the right man for me,' she cut in. 'That was equally bad of you——'

'But that is different.'

'How is it different? You don't know us any more

75

than we know you. You shouldn't go around saying things like that either.'

'If I see them, I must say them. And I see that very clearly——'

'We've only been here a day!' she cut in.

'Yes, and if it is so obvious to me in one short time——'

'I think you've said enough.'

'Then I will say no more. But I have made you think. *That* is enough.' He turned away from her. Casey caught his arm.

'You know, down at the Gallions', I thought you might be quite human after all,' she said. 'Now you're arrogant again—just as I knew you were.'

He looked down at her hand on his arm, smiled slightly, and said, very softly: 'You can be arrogant too, or did you not know that?'

She felt as if her hand was burning, and took it away hastily. 'We'd better go in before we start another quarrel,' she retorted.

'Yes, perhaps we should. Come,' and he pushed open the door. Casey went in, and he followed her. Then they walked in silence to the kitchen, a cool, frosty silence.

Jack was alone, finishing his meal. He was smouldering—that was patently obvious. It was, thought Casey, bemused, like walking out of an ice box into a blaze. He looked up at them, pushed his plate away, and stood up.

'Where the hell have you been?' he demanded.

'Gardening,' she answered. 'Why?' Igor stood just

inside the doorway and folded his arms as if he had decided to be a spectator. Casey looked briefly at him, then back at Jack. Attacks on both sides, she thought. That's all I need.

'Oh yes? I went out looking for you nearly two hours ago," and he consulted his watch in an ostentatious manner, 'and there wasn't a sign of any gardening going on.'

'I'm not surprised,' she answered coolly. 'We were the other side of the wood.'

'The *wood*? What doing—having a picnic?'

She held out her hands. 'Do I look as though I've been on a picnic? I've been working.'

Jack looked at Igor. 'Aren't you going to say anything?' he demanded.

'No.'

'Then why don't you leave us?'

Igor shrugged. 'It is my kitchen. I choose to stay.'

'I suppose you think it's funny coming in two hours late, knowing I'd be worried.'

'We did not know the time. It was only when I saw the clock on the outer wall of the *château* that I realised the hour.' He smiled faintly. 'And as Casey says, we have been working hard. Time passes quickly when you are working—as you must know.' Casey couldn't be sure, but it seemed to her that the Russian's tone was calculated to make Jack even more furious. That it was deliberate she didn't doubt. Igor knew precisely what he was saying, every word carefully honed, his face cool and hard, and the look he gave Jack held just the trace of a faint smile, that

might or might not have been a smirk. 'I did not realise, however,' he continued blandly, 'that she has to
have your consent to be late——' his eyes flickered
across briefly to Casey, and she felt her face tighten,
'she should have told me.'

'I don't,' she said furiously. 'Jack, you're behaving
like a child. I've worked damned hard and I'm tired
and hungry, and I can do without any *more* argu-
ments, thank you,' and she went over to the sink to
wash her hands, then sat down.

'Why? Have you already had one?' Jack looked
furiously at both of them. 'I thought you looked a bit
frosty when you came in—My God, it's this place—
all we seem to do is fight.'

'Shut up!' Casey burst out. 'Leave me alone!'

'What have you done to her?' Jack faced Igor, his
fists clenched.

'Me? Nothing. I do not understand——' his mouth
twitched.

'Oh yes, you damn well do. I'd like to wipe that
smirk off your face——'

'That's enough!' Casey jumped to her feet again and
stood between them. She was shaking with fear and
anger. Fear that Jack might indeed be stupid enough
to try and carry out his threat, and anger with Igor,
who seemed, incredibly, to be the only cool one of the
three. And she suddenly knew why. He was enjoying
himself. She whirled round on him.

'You're a sadist,' she said. 'This suits you, doesn't
it?'

'I don't know what you mean.' But he did. And they both knew why.

'Oh yes, you do. After what you said about Jack——' she stopped, realising the trap. .

'And what did he say about me?' Jack demanded. She had never seen him in such a temper. She had not thought him capable of anything like it.

'Nothing——'

'I will tell him if you like——' began Igor.

'No, you won't. You've done enough,' her eyes flashed fire at him.

Jack pushed Casey to one side. 'Get out of my way.' She stumbled against the table, hitting her side, only slightly, but it was where she had had the pain. Blinded by waves of sickness, she sat in the chair, doubled up, gasping. As Jack, white-faced, moved towards her, Igor grabbed his arms and swung him away. She looked up to see it happen, heard Igor spit out the words:

'Keep away from her——' and then she collapsed, head in hands, unable to move. Whatever might have happened, did not. She felt herself being picked up in a pair of strong arms and being carried out of the kitchen.

When she opened her eyes, she was lying on the long settee in the room of the previous evening. Igor held a glass in his hand. 'Cognac—drink it,' he said.

She looked round. 'Where's Jack? You haven't——'

'No. He is in the kitchen. I am going to talk to him.'

She struggled to sit up. 'Please, don't——'

'Touch him? I will not.' He went out and closed the door. Casey sipped the cognac, and gradually, as the pain in her side subsided, she felt better. Physically better, that is. Mentally she was in turmoil. It had all happened so quickly that she could scarcely remember anything to save a confusion of voices, herself standing between the two men—to protect Jack—of Jack pushing her in his rage. She felt sick, and when the door opened, and she saw Jack, a very chastened Jack, come in, she closed her eyes wearily.

'Casey, I'm sorry,' he began.

She looked at him. 'Sorry for what?'

'Everything. Losing my temper, pushing you—God, I only meant to move you to one side—I didn't know——'

'You wouldn't, I didn't have time to explain anything.' She sipped the cognac and handed him the half empty glass. 'Put this on the table, will you, please? Did he tell you?'

'That you'd hurt your side, yes. He's going to bring your lunch in here in a minute.' He knelt down beside the settee, and put his arms around her. 'Say you'll forgive me?'

'Of course.' She was too weak to say otherwise. And too numb, her senses dulled with the overwhelming events of the day. She just wanted to be left alone. She heard footsteps along the corridor and stiffened. 'Please—don't argue with him again.'

'No, I won't. I had such a scare with you I'm not in any fit state to argue with anyone.' He released her and stood up as Igor came in with a tray.

He looked at Casey. 'Do you feel well enough to eat?' he asked.

'Yes.' She took the tray from him. 'Thanks. I'd rather eat it alone, if you don't mind.'

'Of course.' He glanced briefly at Jack, then went towards the door. After a moment's hesitation Jack followed, and they both went out. Alone, Casey began to eat. She was hungry, and the delicious meaty stew made her feel instantly better. By the time she had finished it, she was back to normal, save for a slight soreness in her side. Getting carefully to her feet, she took the tray out to the kitchen. Igor was alone sitting at the table reading a newspaper and eating his own lunch.

He frowned, stood up and took the tray from her. 'You should not have come in,' he said. 'You should be resting.'

'I'm all right now. Finish your meal. Where's Jack?'

'I don't know.' He shrugged. 'Gone outside for a walk to cool down, I think. Sit down, Casey.'

She sat down at the table. 'Coffee?' he asked.

'Please—white, no sugar.' He stood at the stove and poured coffee into a large cup.

'How is the pain?'

'Nearly gone. Look, Igor, he didn't mean to hurt me——'

'I know. It was me he intended to hurt.' He regarded her coolly across the table. 'And you tried to stop him. For his sake, or mine?'

'Both.' She sipped the hot coffee.

'I would not have been hurt—nor would I have hurt him. I told you that before. I do not fight.'

'You grabbed him——'

'I didn't know what he was going to do.'

She looked at him wide-eyed. 'You didn't think he was going to *hit* me, did you?'

'There was no time to think. I acted instinctively.' He smiled faintly. 'Only his pride was damaged.'

Casey didn't feel like smiling. 'You made it worse,' she accused him, 'by standing there.'

'What would you have had me do? Join in? It is always wiser not to interfere between man and woman.'

'You didn't do so badly, then!' Their eyes met, his dark, shadowed, hers wide.

'Perhaps I had my reasons——'

'Oh yes, and I know what those reasons were.' She put her hand to her forehead and rubbed it.

'Perhaps you do. Do you have a headache?'

'Yes. Is it any wonder, after what's happened?'

'No. You are only a woman, after all——'

'There's no need to be patronising!' she cut in.

'I will get you something. And then you will rest for a while.'

'No. We're going to look at these buildings, and then we're going back to the Gallions'. You said we were.'

'That was before. Besides, I do not think Jack would be pleased.'

'Then let him come with us.'

'You are very determined, Casey.'

'Sometimes I am, yes.' She looked at him. 'Look, I'm fine. My headache will soon be gone—and I want to go back.'

'As you wish. Later today I think you should look at your uncle's papers. It is only right. Everything is ready for you.'

'Yes, I know. Thank you.' She drank the coffee slowly while Igor finished his lunch. She watched him while he ate, saw the high cheekbones, his deep-set eyes, the planes of his face, the implacable strength that lay there, and she closed her eyes, aware of the sheer physical magnetism of the man, despite her personal feelings. There were depths to him that she could not begin to imagine, she knew that. There was nothing shallow or superficial about him; it was as if he vibrated with life and vitality—then he looked up and caught her gaze on him, and for a moment, just a moment, it was as if time stood still, as if, in that instant, there was a deep and frightening awareness, passing from one to the other. Unspoken, as old as time itself, yet it had been, and nothing would ever be the same again.

Casey stood up. 'I'll go and have a wash,' she said, her voice strained even to her own ears. 'Thank you for the coffee.' Quietly, conscious that his eyes stayed upon her, she walked out of the room.

Everything had changed. Most subtly, and in a way Casey could not begin to define, everything was—different. It was as if there were a clarity and sharpness to the whole world that had not been before. As if she could see everything more clearly. And when, a short time after, she saw Igor walking towards her from the *château*, she watched him come and it seemed that she saw him through different eyes. Jack, sitting beside her on the grass, looked up. The shock of what had happened in the kitchen was nearly forgotten; he was back to normal, Casey could tell. I wish I was, she thought. I don't even know what's the matter with me.

'Ready?' asked Igor. He carried a basket containing meat and vegetables. Jack had apparently come to the conclusion that it might be better to try and get on with Igor. It was almost transparently obvious in the way he answered him. Perhaps, thought Casey shrewdly, he's realised just how near he was to having a fight with someone who could easily have killed him.

'Do you want to go in our car?' Jack asked.

'It is impossible. We go through the woods. There is no road to the Gallions', only a track.'

Jack dusted some dry earth from his trousers. It was also obvious, to Casey at least, that he didn't want to go to the Gallion family's house. She sighed. He's only going because he resents us being alone together —and I can't say I blame him, she thought wryly— and he'd really rather be working on his stuffy old blueprints in his bedroom. There was in fact a faintly martyred air about him as he walked along beside Casey towards the trees. She was very determined that there would be no quarrels, no disagreements, nothing

to mar the afternoon. Apart from any other considera-
tion, she didn't feel as if she could take any more. She
began therefore to explain some of the situation regarding the family they were going to, and Jack asked
all the right questions in the right places, but she
thought suddenly in the middle of one of his answers:
he doesn't really care. There was a lack of any warmth
to his voice. It was almost as if he said—I don't know
why you're bothering, it's no concern of ours.

She also made a discovery about him at that moment. She had known it subconsciously all along, yet
had preferred to ignore it. He only ever made an effort
with people if they could be of use to him. He uses
people, she thought. He always has, and he can't see
why I or anyone else should bother with a poor family
who need help. She wondered if Igor was aware of anything, and glanced quickly at him. He loped along,
apparently lost in thought, probably not even listening
—yet she knew that he was, that nothing ever escaped
him. That was something she had sensed instinctively
about him. It was almost frightening to feel she knew
so much about a man who was a virtual stranger—a
man she had met for the first time less than twenty-
four hours previously. And she had met Jack over a
year ago, and knew him scarcely at all.

'Sorry?' She hadn't been listening. Jack had just
asked a question, only now Igor was answering him.

'Casey feels they might be better living by the *château*,' he said. 'Which is why she is going to talk to
Madame Gallion today.'

'What?' Jack looked at her as if she were mad. 'In the *château*?'

'No. There are some stables at the back——'

'And that's your idea? You can't just go around inviting everybody to move in, you know——'

'I'm not,' she answered calmly. 'It was only a suggestion. Haven't you been listening at all?'

'Of course I have. You want to help this family—well, good for you, but there is a limit, you know.'

She looked at Igor. For once she didn't know what to say. She saw him smile faintly, and she thought, yes, damn you, you're enjoying this again.

'I think the idea is sound,' answered Igor in level tones. 'But as I explained to Casey, it is not so simple as she would make it appear.'

'All right, I know, I know,' she answered. 'I rush into things without thinking—don't say it.'

'You do have that tendency,' Jack agreed. Then to Igor: 'She's always finding stray animals, and then having to hunt around for homes for them. I've told her many a time—do you remember that kitten that ripped your curtains?'

'It would have got run over if I hadn't taken it home,' she said, forgetting the interested audience of one in her indignation. 'I couldn't leave it in the middle of that road, could I? Anyway, they were *my* curtains. I didn't ask you to pay for their repair——'

'That's not the point. All you needed to do was take it to the police station——'

'Oh yes! And they'd have had it put down after a

couple of days. Anyway, Barbara had it in the end, and it's a gorgeous big creature now——'

'That dog wasn't. It's a wonder it wasn't riddled with fleas—I wouldn't be surprised if it was. God knows how you managed to persuade Dobbs to turn a blind eye while you smuggled it in—huge mangy animal——'

She stopped in her tracks. 'Don't you like dogs? You never said before.'

'Sure I like them—in their place, and clean ones, not——'

'I'm sure Igor's not interested, Jack. Hadn't we better change the subject?'

'No. Please do go on,' Igor said politely. 'What happened to this dog?'

She stared hard at him, trying to detect sarcasm. There appeared to be none. 'I found it a home—eventually,' she said. 'And it was nice and clean when it went——'

'But your bath will never be the same again,' Jack cut in.

She ignored that. 'He's now being spoiled in a children's home that a friend of mine works at.' She turned to Jack. 'Anyway, Igor looks after a wild goose with a broken wing, don't you, Igor?'

It was as if Jack realised, suddenly, that he might have been a little more sympathetic. Casey felt almost sorry for him. There was a brief, rather full silence, then Igor spoke.

'Somebody has to keep an eye on it,' he said mildly. 'Tell me, Jack, about your work. You have some plans you are making at the moment?'

He had deliberately changed the subject, and Casey wondered why. She also wondered why he was being nice to Jack, after what had happened. She was sure, in her intuitive way, that he did nothing without a purpose.

Their conversation washed over her. She had heard it all before—what interested her more was Igor's possible motive when he so clearly disliked Jack. Yet to hear them now, no one would have known. It made her more than a little uneasy.

That evening Casey sat in the kitchen peeling potatoes while Boris, at the other side of the table, diced onions and mushrooms. With him she felt truly relaxed, and it was one reason why she had gone in to offer her help. The other reason was that both Jack and Igor had disappeared, Jack to drive down to the village to telephone a colleague in London, Igor to water the plants. It was dark outside, the lights were on, and the kitchen was pleasantly cool after the heat of the day. The two dogs slumbered on their mat by the window, all was peaceful.

'You are kind to help,' remarked Boris after a long companionable silence.

Casey looked up, lost in thought. 'I enjoy preparing meals,' she answered. 'I thought I might learn something from you. You're a very good cook.'

He smiled disarmingly. 'I do as best I can. Perhaps we will do some Russian meals while you are here. Would you like that?'

'Of course.' She sniffed. Some meat was simmering in an enormous pan on the stove. 'I'm starving!'

'You have been working hard, that is why. It is good to eat after a day's work. Now, you have done the potatoes, for which I thank you. There is a bowl of strawberries to be cleaned and prepared, if you would be so kind. Over there on the cupboard.' She went over to the antique dresser and lifted the heavy bowl, taking it back to the table, and the door opened and Igor came in.

'We will eat in the dining room tonight, Boris,' he said. 'It might be nice to let our guests know that we are civilised.'

'Of course.' Boris nodded and padded quietly out. Igor turned to Casey. She felt her heartbeats quicken, and lifted the plate from off the top of the bowl, as if the strawberries were all-important.

'I wish to speak to you,' he said.

'Well, you are doing,' she pointed out, reasonably enough, she thought.

'In private. Later.'

'What about?'

'Several things. Things that concern you and me only.'

'What you mean is—without Jack.'

'If you like, yes.'

'That could be difficult.' She smiled. 'After this afternoon I hardly think he's going to let me out of his sight for very long, do you?'

'That is why I am speaking to you now, while he is away. He wants to work on his plans—I know that. If you say you are tired and are going to bed he will probably go up to his room and stay there. Then we can discuss what we have to.'

'In my room! You must be——'

He made a dismissive gesture with his hand. 'No. You can come down, of course.'

'And if *he* comes down for anything, what then? He wouldn't be very pleased.'

'Then I will tell him the truth. There's not much he can do about that. But it is unlikely.'

'All right.' She was busily taking off the tops of the strawberries as she spoke, and Igor reached over and took one, his hand brushing hers for a second. It was like receiving an electric shock . . . 'Just give me an idea why all this secrecy. I told you all that happened at Madame Gallion's, and it was little——' she paused. She had not told him everything, but now was not the time.

'This does not concern the family Gallion. Although I sense your fiancé thinks we are quite mad to wish to help—it concerns you only—and me——' he stopped as Boris came back into the room. 'I am going to bathe and change now.' With a last look at Casey, he went out.

She stared at the table, seeing nothing save his face. A pulse beat in her throat, and a small inner sense of excitement filled her. She could not explain it, nor did she want to. She only knew that since the morning her feelings had been in a turmoil. And all because of one man—Igor Borodinov. And what on earth could he wish to say that was so private?

CHAPTER SIX

I⊤ all went according to plan. At least the first part did. After dinner when they went to drink coffee in the sitting room, Casey yawned and looked at Jack. 'I think I'll have an early night,' she said. 'I'm exhausted.' It was the perfect truth. She was in fact very tired, and knew she looked it.

'I'll probably go up too,' he said. 'I phoned George—and now I want to iron out some snags. I'll walk up with you.'

Igor had been standing by the window. 'Goodnight,' he said.

'Goodnight,' answered Jack. Casey didn't. She felt guiltily as though it would be compounding the lie if she did.

At the top of the stairs, Jack took her in his arms. 'Oh, Casey,' he groaned. 'We don't seem to have had any time alone since we set out from London.' He kissed her eagerly, and Casey tried to respond with enthusiasm—but in vain. He stood away for a moment.

'Hey, what's up?'

'Nothing—I guess I'm too tired, love. Sorry.'

'Hmm,' he began to stroke the back of her neck. 'Why don't you come up to my room for five minutes? There's hardly any privacy here.'

'Because it wouldn't be five minutes, would it? It

would be an hour.' She smiled at him, yet inside she felt wretched at the deception.

'True,' he admitted. 'But damn it all, we've had no time alone——'

'It's only for a short while. When we're back in London——'

'You mean we're not staying?' His face brightened.

She wasn't sure what she had meant. 'No—well, only for a week or so—at least——' she frowned. 'Oh, I don't know, Jack. I'm too tired to think straight.'

He sighed. 'You look it. All right, off you go. See you in the morning—g'night, my darling.'

'Goodnight, Jack.' She watched him run up the staircase that led to his room, then went on to her own. After washing her face and hands in the ancient, cracked basin in the corner of her room, she went and lay down on the bed, simply to give Jack time to start work before she went down again. She didn't even intend to close her eyes, but she did. And two minutes later she was fast asleep . . .

An urgent rapping at the door roused her. For a moment she didn't know where she was, then sitting up, she said: 'Come in.'

It was Igor who entered, closed the door, and said: 'I thought you were coming down.'

She stared at him blankly. 'I must have fallen asleep—I'm sorry.'

'No matter. We can talk here. It will not take long.'

'I'd rather not——' she began.

He came over to the bed and sat down on it. 'Why? You are quite safe.'

'Am I?'

He regarded her very levelly from the depths of those dark eyes. Then he smiled. 'I give you my word.'

Casey nodded. 'All right. What is it you want to say?'

'Just these few things. This *château* belongs equally to you and to me. That is a fact of which we are both aware, no? And Jack wishes you to sell your half —but his opinion must be of no importance to us. I also would like that—and I want you to think about it and let me know what you decide soon.'

'Why?' she asked bluntly.

'Because——' he shrugged. 'Because it is important to me. There is much work to be done—you must have seen that for yourself—and I am prepared to do most of it—and I would like to open it as an hotel.'

'What? An *hotel*! Are you mad?'

'No. Do I strike you as unbalanced?'

She was tempted to answer yes, if only to see his reaction. And when she had first met him, had he told her what he just had, she would indeed have been in-clined to think so. But in the one day she had known him all her opinions had been turned topsy-turvy. He was probably the most level-headed man she had ever met. Forceful, aggressive—and with that restless energy which could well mean success in anything he chose to do. And yet, in an odd way, his words had given her a shock.

'No, I'm sure you're not,' she answered slowly. 'But I can't take this in—not yet anyway.'

'That is why I wished to tell you tonight. Alone, so that you could think over what I say. It was your uncle's wish too. He talked over the idea many times, and it appealed very much to him, but his health was failing, and——' he shrugged, 'nothing came of it.' He looked at Casey. 'So in a way, it would be carrying out his wish if I should do so.' The subtle moral blackmail wasn't lost on her, and she glanced at him, and it showed in her eyes. She saw him catch his breath.

'You're clever,' she said very quietly. 'I'll hand you that.'

He nodded an acknowledgement. 'Then we understand each other?'

She paused before she answered. 'I think we have right from the beginning.' The undercurrents of mounting tension were in the air, subtle and undefined, for Casey.

'Perhaps,' he said slowly, 'because we are two of a kind.'

'No!' The word came out sharply—too sharply. 'I'm not like you——'

'Yes, I think you are. You are as determined as I——'

'I'm different.' She stared wide-eyed at him.

'You are a woman, I am a man. And we speak a different mother tongue. In those respects, yes, we are different. But in others——' he paused, and his eyes seemed to be absorbing her into him so that she felt weak and helpless. Casey tried to look away, but found it impossible.

'Stop it!' she cried, the words wrenched out of her, and she hardly knew why she said them.

Igor put his hand on hers. 'But I am not doing any-thing——'

'Yes, you are!' She felt stifled. 'Don't touch me!'

He took his hand away. 'Do I frighten you so much?'

'Yes—no——'

'I do not mean to. It is yourself you are frightened of. Do you not know that, Casey?'

'Don't be silly!' she tried a laugh, which didn't quite come off. 'How can anyone be frightened of themselves?' She swung her legs to the floor and moved away from him. Anywhere to have a safe dis-tance between them. From the window she turned and looked at him. 'Perhaps you'd better go now.'

He rose slowly to his feet and came towards her. Casey backed away, stupidly, she knew, but she couldn't help it. Igor saw, and he knew, and he stop-ped, just feet away.

'I was not going to touch you,' he said. 'Did you think I was?'

'How can I know, with you?' she said. 'I don't know what you'll do from one minute to the next. I told you I didn't want to talk here—I would have come down——' she felt as if she was babbling again.

'Then had you not better come down now anyway? I have the papers of your uncle for you to go over. You will feel safe there. And you can have a drink to steady your nerves——'

'I don't need a drink, thank you. There's nothing

wrong with my nerves—it's my muscles that are aching if anything, thanks to the gardening——'

'Ah yes. And the pain in your side, how is that?'

'I'll live.'

'Has it not gone?'

'No. But it's all right. I'll rub it—I know what to do now.'

'Shall I?'

'No!' Then she saw the hidden laughter in his eyes, and felt angry. He had said it deliberately, knowing her reaction. Eyes blazing, she said accusingly: 'You said that on purpose, didn't you?'

She had expected him to deny it. She should have known better. 'Yes, of course. To see what you would do. You run from me like a frightened goose——'

'And you enjoy that, don't you? I told you you were a sadist, and you are.'

'A harsh way to describe me, Casey. Is that how you really see me?'

'In some ways, yes. You have a cruel streak in you——'

'No.'

'Yes!'

'Then perhaps you have too—or why else would you have told Jack that I looked after an injured wild goose just after he had been making clear his opinion of people who found lost animals?'

'I thought we'd agreed to leave my fiancé out of this,' she said, with dignity.

'It is very difficult, though. He is here, after all, and

clearly you let yourself be influenced a lot by him, which is why I had to talk to you alone——'

'I don't,' she denied. 'I would have come here on my own——'

'But you didn't. Do you really love him?'

She stared at him. 'Of *course* I—that has nothing to do with you. You have no right to ask such a personal question anyway——'

'I told you once before, I ask you anything I like. *You* have the right to refuse to answer if you don't wish to. That is fair.'

'That is not exactly the point,' she answered, exasperated. 'It's embarrassing for people to be asked that by perfect strangers.'

'But we are not perfect strangers, are we?' And the room went very still. It was almost as if time itself had stopped, and was waiting, waiting . . .

Casey looked into Igor's face. 'What—what do you mean?' she whispered, fearful of breaking the spell that seemed to hold them in a timeless web.

'You already know, I think. There are some people we can know all our lives and yet remain strangers to, and there are others who meet for the first time—and it is as if they have known each other before, in some different place, and——'

'No. You're talking nonsense——' but she knew, even as she said it, that it was not so. Yet some force within her compelled her to deny his words, and the strength with which he said them. She whirled away from him to go towards the door, and he caught her with all his considerable power, caught and held her, and she could not escape.

'Yes,' he said, 'and you are denying what you know is the truth——'

'No, leave me——' she struggled vainly. 'You promised you wouldn't touch me——'

'Then admit what I say is true.'

She looked up at him, pleading for release, and all her spirit was in her eyes and her lips trembled help-lessly. With a groan he let her go, and she would have fallen had he not steadied her. Casey collapsed on to the bed, rubbing her arms, too shaken to speak. Igor bent and lifted her up—very gently. She began to cry. Softly he held her, cradling her in his arms like a child, stroking her hair.

'Forgive me,' he said. 'Don't cry.'

'You frightened me,' she whispered.

'It was not my intention.'

'It was. It was. You knew what you were doing——'

'Yes, I did,' he murmured. 'I knew exactly what I was doing.'

'Then why——?' She knew she shouldn't be in his arms, that it was completely wrong, that she ought to be pushing him away, but for the life of her she couldn't. She didn't even want to, and that was worse.

'Because, little wild goose, that is the effect you have on me.'

Then she found the strength to free herself. She pulled herself away, and there was no resistance on his part. White-faced and trembling, she stared at him.

'Please go now,' she said.

'I think it better I should,' his voice was harsh and deep. He turned away and went out, leaving her standing alone in the room. His footsteps died away into the silence. Very slowly, Casey went over and locked the door. Then she began to prepare for bed.

When she woke the next morning, she was aching in every muscle. It was even an effort to sit up in bed. The late morning sun streamed through the open window and she moved her arm, wincing slightly, and looked at her watch. It was nearly noon. She could hear no sounds from anywhere in the *château*, only birds singing outside. The memories came flooding back, but she deliberately pushed them away and got out of bed.

When she went down at last, dressed in jeans and white figure-hugging cotton sweater, she made a bee-line for the kitchen. She was starving. Igor was there alone. She hesitated in the doorway and he turned and looked at her.

'Good morning, Casey.'

'Good morning. Where's Jack—and Boris?' He was pouring coffee out and handed her a beakerful before replying.

'Boris is down at the village for food. Jack has gone riding with a friend of mine. He asked me to tell you.'

'Oh.' She felt as though she had missed something important, like a piece out of a jigsaw. 'Er—when did they go?'

'An hour ago. He waited for you and then decided it might be best if you slept on. You were so tired last night.' It was as if their conversation hadn't happened. His manner was quite impersonal.

'Would you like some breakfast?'

'Well, it's so late. Can I have just a piece of toast?'

'Of course.'

'I'll do it——' she began.

'Sit and drink your coffee. It won't take me a moment.'

She watched him cutting bread and switching on the grill. He wore jeans and a grey short-sleeved shirt, the thin fabric of which was stretched tautly over his broad back and shoulders. He was, as usual, barefoot.

'There you are.' He pushed the dish of butter towards her as he handed her the plate of toast, then sat down himself, with his coffee. 'You slept well?'

'Fairly well. I ache. I'm not used to gardening—but it'll pass.' She bit into the crunchy toast. At least he didn't put her off her food.

'Have you thought about my suggestion?' For a moment she didn't understand the question, and had a mild inward panic. Perhaps he sensed it, for he added: 'About the hotel?'

'Oh. No, not yet. I was too tired.'

'But you will?'

'Yes, I will.' She looked at him, and it was difficult to meet his eyes. Things had been said the previous night that were better forgotten. Shatteringly personal things, touching on a deep level of awareness that had frightened her, and even now, in the cold light of day, could return to disturb her if she let them. 'I promise.' She began to feel uneasy. 'Are you going to see the Gallions today?' There was safe ground.

'No. The children will come soon, I am sure. They are here nearly every day.'

'You don't mind?'

He shrugged. 'Mind? No. I like children.' It was not a thing a man usually admitted, unless they were his own. Jack didn't. He felt awkward with them, he had once told Casey, and she had never forgotten it. Igor spoke so casually that she had to smile.

'You find it amusing?'

'No, of course not. Only—well, men don't usually.'

'Why not? They see things differently. The children interest me, especially Emil. One day I shall get him to talk.' He said it with such a quiet assurance that Casey felt moved.

'I hope you do. You told me that when you pulled him out of the lake, you also found the injured goose. Do you think—could there be any connection?'

'In what way?' he frowned. 'You think *he* hurt it?'

'Oh no,' she was shocked. 'No, I meant—could he have seen it, perhaps, and been trying to rescue it?'

'Possibly. Who can know now? Marie was there as well. I heard her shouting for help too—she never mentioned it, and I will not remind them of it. And I prefer you do not either.'

'Of course I wouldn't. Have *you* thought any more about my suggestion?'

'Regarding the Gallions? Come, we will go and look

at the buildings now.' He stood up. 'Better perhaps to do that while Jack is out?'

'I suppose so—look, Igor, don't get him wrong. He just thought——'

'Of course,' Igor raised an amused eyebrow. 'He was looking after your interests, that is all. Come, this way.'

He led her out of another door, and along a passage to the back of the *château*. Outside was a cobbled square, like an enclosed courtyard surrounded by buildings. He pointed. 'Over there. Are those the ones you mean?'

'I think so.' She looked around her doubtfully. 'There are more than I remembered——'

'Then we will look around them all. Come.' He took her arm and led her across the dry cobbles towards the nearest door. Inside the roomy stable it was cool and shadowy, with the faintest lingering traces of old hay scenting the air. There were no windows, only a skylight in the roof.

'No, this isn't the one.'

They went out and along the cobbles again and he pushed open another door. This was smaller, with rooms leading off the main one, and it had been used for storing paint and tools from what remained. There were windows. 'Oh yes,' Casey said, 'this has possibilities. Look——' she pointed, 'it only needs doors fitting——'

'Yes, that could be done. But Madame Gallion was not very interested when you suggested it.'

Casey looked at him. 'I didn't tell you. She's expecting another child. She hasn't told anyone yet, only me.' She looked at him. 'She's managed to keep the fact from her husband so far—but when he does find out, do you think he's going to be pleased? We *must* do something for them.'

'Oh no.' Igor shook his head. 'Why did you not tell me yesterday?'

'I couldn't. She—she asked me not to. She's frightened, Igor—that's why I've told you now.' She bit her lip. 'Soon—he's going to know——'

'Yes. I will go later today and talk to them.'

'Shall I come with you?'

He regarded her thoughtfully. 'I don't know——'

'I can help. At least I can try—or I can keep the children out of the way, in the garden, while you talk.'

'And Jack? What of him? He might not——'

'I'll deal with him,' she said.

Igor's mouth twitched. 'Are you sure?'

'He's gone off riding, hasn't he? Without me?' She frowned. 'Who's the friend, anyway? Does he live near—do *you* go riding with him?'

There was a brief pause, and it seemed that Igor might be trying not to laugh. 'Ah,' he said at last. 'Near enough. You might say we are neighbours. My friend has a rather beautiful villa nearby—but it is not "he" but "she". She is an Italian *contessa*, a widow.'

Casey opened her mouth to speak, and no words came. Igor added helpfully: 'She is about thirty-five— much older than you.'

'A *contessa*,' she said, because for the moment it was the only thing she could say.

'Yes. You will meet her soon. I dare say they will be back shortly.' He took Casey's arm in the gentlest possible manner. 'I know she is thinking of having some alterations done to her villa. Perhaps Jack will be able to make a few suggestions?'

She shook her arm free, a deep and growing suspicion within her. He was being far too casual—and was he, ever so slightly, enjoying himself? 'How strange,' she said coolly, 'that she should arrive this morning.'

'Yes, isn't it?' He looked blandly at her.

'You didn't know she was coming?'

He shrugged. 'How could I know? She turns up—it is very casual. She is rather lonely, I think.'

'Oh, really?' she didn't try to hide the sarcasm. 'A rich Italian *contessa*, lonely?' She was furious—but not in the way she thought she would be, once the initial shock had worn off. Her fury was for Igor, not Jack— which was most odd, and she would have to think about it later.

'Did I say she was rich? Well, she may be. It is not a thing that I concern myself with. Friends are friends, it is as simple as that——'

'Then how much of a "friend" is she?'

'A good one.' And he smiled. It was the smile that did it. More than his words, more than anything else. Casey didn't think about what she was doing, or why she was doing it—or the warning she had had. She simply hit him hard.

There was a frozen instant of silence, then: 'I told you—never hit me again!' he breathed—then she was in his arms. But now it was different from the times before. Now it was oh, so different. For when Igor kissed her, it was no savage punishment, it was the deep kiss of a man for a woman. A deep, satisfying everlasting kiss that rocked her from top to toe, left her weak and breathless—she put her arms round his neck, and the second one was infinitely more satisfying than the first and there was going to be no end to it . . .

'Igor, *mio caro*, you are here——' the deep velvety voice came from the door, and they spun apart, Casey dizzily aware of the slender black-haired beauty standing languidly in the doorway. Then she laughed.

'Hello! And you must be Casey?' She moved gracefully forward. It was as if she had seen nothing, for her voice was as fresh and innocent as the morning as she shook hands with Casey. 'Your fiancé'—there was only the subtlest touch of irony in the word—'is looking for you in the *château*. I said I would come out here to water the horses.' She turned limpid eyes to Igor. 'He has been *so* helpful. But now I am dying of thirst. Are you going to be the good host and look after me?'

'Of course.' He bent and kissed her cheek. 'We will go back now.' He took her arm, leaving Casey to follow. Had she seen? More important—would she tell? Casey was in an agony as she walked back across the cobbles, seeing without really noticing the two gorgeous horses drinking water at a stone trough. She had been stupid and impetuous, and nothing was going to undo what had happened—but she wished desperately that it hadn't. Tensely she went in, lagging deliberately a few steps behind, and Jack came along the passage from the kitchen.

'There you are,' he said. 'I was shouting the place down.'

'We went to see the stables,' Igor said calmly, 'and then Lucia came round with the horses.'

The two men walked on into the kitchen, and the Contessa took Casey's arm. 'He is so nice, your Jack,' she said sweetly. 'It was kind of you to let me borrow him for an hour.'

Borrow? She made him sound like a pound bag of sugar. Casey looked at her. How did you say—please don't tell Jack that we were kissing, because it was all a terrible mistake and only happened because I'd hit him—and the reason I hit him was because I was jealous, but I'm not sure whether I was jealous of him being your friend or Jack being out with you—but I've got a good idea which? There was no possible way to do so. 'I'm sure he enjoyed the ride, Contessa,' she said.

'Oh, please call me Lucia. Everyone does. Titles are so old-fashioned, do you not think?'

Hmm, I'll bet you wouldn't relinquish yours in a hurry, thought Casey.

'Thank you, you're very kind,' she said instead.

Jack and Igor were waiting in the lounge as Lucia sailed in followed by Casey, who had opportunity to look at her properly for the first time. She was beautiful, no mistake about that. Slender, with a mass of dark hair tumbling, oh, so casually round her shoulders, a small pointed face with huge dark eyes and deep red lips. The fawn jodhpurs she wore fitted her to perfection, and the casual simplicity of her yellow silk shirt spoke of wealth. She moved elegantly, fully conscious of the effect she made, and took the glass from Igor with the words: 'You always know exactly how I like my vodka, *caro*—just the merest whisper of Martini.' She went and sat beside Jack on the settee. 'So you think those extra bedrooms could be added quite easily without spoiling the line of the house?'

Casey only half heard. Igor was asking her what she wanted. She went over to him, and she knew now why he had asked so many questions of Jack the previous day about his work. She knew there had been a reason. She didn't know how he had got in touch with Lucia, for there was no telephone at the *château*, but she was willing to gamble her last shilling that he had done so—somehow. But why?

'Kirsch for me, please.' Their eyes met. His were giving nothing away. Casey suddenly felt as if she were part of some shabby conspiracy. It was not a pleasant feeling to have.

'You'll stay for lunch, Lucia?' asked Igor.

'Oh, I can't, darling. I have some friends coming over this afternoon from Monte Carlo.' She gave Jack a winning smile. 'Such a bore! Business friends of my late husband's. He's quite pleasant, but his wife is a dowdy woman,' she shuddered. 'Why don't you three come over? It would liven the place up?' She looked appealingly at the two men—but not at all at Casey.

'I can't, I have work to do,' replied Igor smoothly. He's different with her, Casey thought in wonder. It's as though he belongs in her crowd—a part of it. It was most odd. He looked at Jack. 'But you and Casey must go, of course, if you want.'

'What about it, Casey?' Jack too was different. Perhaps she has this effect on men, thought Casey sourly. And I'm sure I don't care.

'I'm going to go through some papers of my late uncle's,' she answered. It was partly true anyway, and she didn't feel inclined to mention their planned visit to the Gallions'. Jack said nothing, but she saw the flash of disappointment—that could so easily turn to sulking—in his eyes.

'You go, Jack,' she urged him. 'I'm sure you'd be bored looking through a pile of old letters and things with me.'

There was a pregnant silence, then Lucia put a small neat hand on Jack's arm. 'My dear,' she said, 'what fun—would you like to come?'

'Well——' he hesitated, but it was obvious, to Casey anyway, that he'd already decided. 'If you're sure, Casey——' he looked at her, a boyish smile on his face.

'Of course I'm sure.'

'Then that's settled. And I will stay to lunch, Igor, then Jack and I can ride over together right afterwards.' Lucia turned to Casey as Igor left the room, presumably to tell Boris. 'Jack was telling me you have a flat in the heart of London? My dear, how marvellous! I love London——' she prattled on pleasantly, and Casey watched her. She looks, she thought, like the cat that's found the cream. She looks as if this is precisely what she wanted to happen. But if so—why? She nodded and answered Lucia's questions with only half a mind on them. The other half was working furiously. One question was uppermost. If she had seen us—and Casey was certain she had—what will she be thinking? Casey had a good idea, which was why she was beginning to feel less hungry by the minute.

They had gone, and she and Igor were alone again. The whole atmosphere changed with their departure, and Casey moved restlessly to the window, to see Lucia and Jack cantering off into the distance.

'It will be late before he returns,' he said, and he was watching her. It was the first time they had been alone since that never-to-be-forgotten kiss in the stable.

Casey turned away. 'I imagine it will.'

'Do you mind?'

'I don't know. Igor, I want to explain——'

'About what?'

'B-before—in the stable—I—was angry——'

'I know. With me—or yourself?'

'With you.'

'Because Jack had gone with Lucia, and you suspected I had planned it—or because I said she was my friend?'

'I—don't know.'

'Then I suggest you forget it. It is better. Never look back, Casey.'

She turned to look at him. 'You make things sound so *easy*, don't you?' she said bitterly.

'Sometimes it helps.'

'Oh!' she clasped her hands. 'I feel—so mixed up.'

'Then stop thinking of yourself for a change—remember where we are going instead. And plan what you want to say.'

He was only inches away from her. She let out her breath. 'I suppose you're right. I—I'm sorry I hit you.'

'Are you? And you want me to say I'm sorry for kissing you?' He smiled faintly. 'If so, you will be disappointed.' He touched her arm. 'Come, it is time we went.'

CHAPTER SEVEN

THEN, slowly and inexorably, as if the threads in some giant tapestry were being woven into their place, came the next event, and it was in a way one that overshadowed all that had gone before—but in another way was part of it all.

It began as they were nearly at the Gallions' house. They could see it in the distance, and it had a deserted air about it, as if abandoned, and nothing moved. The door was closed. Igor looked at Casey, and frowned.

'Perhaps they've gone out,' she suggested, but a sense of foreboding filled her.

'I don't know.' He ran the last few yards, and knocked on the door, Casey behind him. 'Madame Gallion?' he called.

There was silence, and Casey felt the hairs prickle at the back of her neck. He turned the door handle, and went into the small living room. A child whimpered, something moved in the corner, and Marie got up from where she had been crouching with her brother and sister, and stumbled towards them.

'Marie,' Igor bent down to her level, 'what is it? Where is your mother?'

'I thought you were Papa.' She was crying, and had been for a while, the tears coursing down her cheeks, her eyes red and sore. Igor held her closely.

'It is me. Stop crying—where is she?'

'In bed. She is poorly.' He turned and looked at Casey. 'Go and see. Quickly! Through there.' He pointed to a closed door, then went over to where Emil and his sister lay on a mattress and knelt down. Casey did as she was told, tapping on the bedroom door. Then she opened it and went in. Madame Gallion lay on her side in bed, and one look at her deathly white face and the bruises which covered it were enough to tell Casey that the woman was very ill.

She went over to her and took her hand. 'Madame, it is me—Casey—we are here to help you. What happened?'

Her eyes were glazed and blank, yet there was an almost reassuring pressure as she gripped Casey's hand tightly in return. 'Marie and Emil—are they well?' she whispered. 'And the baby?'

'Yes. Igor is with them. We must get you a doctor. Don't talk now——'

'He beat us—he knew you had been here again—and when I would not tell him why——' she paused, shuddering.

'Please don't talk. I'll get you a drink.' Casey went out to Igor, who stood up. 'She's been beaten, Igor. She needs a doctor urgently.'

'So do the kids.' He nodded towards them sitting on the mattress, his face holding an anger she had never seen before. 'I'm going down to the village to fetch him. You must lock the door, and if *he* comes back, don't let him in. You understand? I'll be as quick as

I can.' He took her arm and led her towards the outer door. There was a large bolt on it. 'Lock it now. I'll shout when I come back. Until I do, look after them. Make some coffee—anything you can find. But don't open the door.'

'No, I won't. Hurry!' She almost pushed him out, and slammed the bolt to. Then she went to find a kettle and water.

Casey had brought a bowl into the bedroom, after putting the baby, Annette, in beside her mother, and was bathing the child's face when there was a thunderous knocking at the outer door, and Igor's voice came: 'Casey? Let us in, please.'

She put the bowl of water on the floor and smiled reassuringly at Madame Gallion. 'He's back now.'

'Don't leave us—please, don't go away.' She clutched Casey's hand, her eyes wide and frightened.

'We won't, I promise you,' Casey assured her. 'After the doctor has seen you, you're coming back to the *château* with us.' She quickly left them and opened the front door for Igor and a small middle-aged man, who nodded briskly, said: '*Bonjour, mademoiselle*,' and vanished into the bedroom.

Igor spoke quietly. 'We've come back in Doctor Gilles' car from the village. If she's well enough to be moved he's prepared to drive us back and along to the *château*.'

'And if she's not?'

'Then we stay.'

'Are there any hospitals?'

'There's one about fifteen kilometres away—you think——?' he stopped.

'I think she might have lost the baby, yes.'

He drew in his breath sharply. 'That decides it. She is leaving here——'

'I think she knows she must.' Casey was filled with an inner strength now. 'I'll go and wash the children.' She went over to them and spoke in French. 'Come to the kitchen, and I will make you nice and clean,'

She heard the doctor come out from the bedroom while she was busy scrubbing Emil's legs with a face cloth, heard the two men speaking with low voices but couldn't catch any words. She smiled reassuringly at them both.

'Would you like to stay at the *château* for a while?'

Marie nodded. 'Will Papa be there?'

'I think not. Will you mind?'

The little girl shrugged. 'He is not kind to us.'

'He is sick, Marie, he needs treatment. Perhaps he will get it——'

'If M'sieur Igor is there it will be good. We can help in the gardens?'

'Of course.' She dried Emil's legs. 'There, that's all done. You both look nice and clean. Come on.' So much for her concern. Marie's realistic outlook effectively solved any problem. As long as M'sieur Igor was there, all would be well.

They were waiting for her. She should have known what was to come. Yet perhaps in a way she had all along, ever since first entering the house that day. Igor looked at her. 'Doctor Gilles says that Madame Gallion will need nursing for a few days. She must either go to the hospital——' he paused.

'Or I can do it? Yes.' Casey smiled. 'I think I knew already. Of course I will. I'll do anything to help.' She turned to the doctor and went on in French: 'Will you tell me precisely what I have to do, doctor?'

'She will need constant care for several days, *mademoiselle*. It needs only common sense—and a lot of your time. I will be pleased to tell you when we are back at the *château*. Meanwhile, the sooner we depart, the better, I think. I have sedated Madame, and there are certain medicines I must get for her.' He looked at Igor. 'Monsieur Borodinov, can you carry Madame Gallion? She is well wrapped in blankets, and my car is ready.'

Then, before Igor could reply, the door from outside was pushed open—and a man stood in the doorway, a big man, dark and unshaven and the worse for drink. Casey, acting swiftly, grabbed Emil's and Marie's hands and pulled them. 'Come into the bedroom,' she said. She closed the door after them and stood just outside it. He gets in over my dead body, she thought, with an icy cold determination.

The little tableau would be for ever etched in her mind. The doctor, pausing as he was about to put stethescope back in his bag, Igor turning slowly towards the door, and the man, swaying slightly as he surveyed them, his face black with anger.

'What goes on?' he said. 'What are you doing in my house?' His voice was slurred.

'Looking after your wife,' replied Igor with deceptive mildness. He didn't look remotely angry—yet. 'She is very ill—thanks to you. And now she is going with us to where she can be cared for properly. So if you wouldn't mind moving out of the doorway——'

'Like hell she is! She stays here—with me.'

Doctor Gilles spoke then. 'You have no choice, Monsieur Gallion. It is either that or we call the police——'

'The police! Pah!' he spat. 'The *flics* know enough to keep away from me.'

'They don't like child-beaters any more than I do,' said Igor with deadly calm. 'And if you don't get out of my way you'll find out how much I don't like you.' He moved quietly towards the other man. Jean Gallion lurched forward, arms swinging, and Igor chopped him at the side of the neck. It was over in a second. The big man fell, and Igor dragged him over to the mattress in the corner and dumped him on it like a sack of potatoes.

'Get the three children out,' he said to Casey, 'and take them to the car. I'll fetch their mother.'

Ten minutes later they were driving down a narrow twisted track to the village in the doctor's battered Citröen.

Boris was the surprising one, thought Casey several hours later as she sat with her feet up, having a most welcome five-minute break with a cup of hot coffee.

It was as if coping with four unexpected guests was an everyday occurrence. He had prepared three bedrooms on the first floor with all speed, and Madame Gallion was installed in the first while he got on with the other two, one for Casey, the other for the children. Then he had made them all a meal, and had told Casey to rest while he took it in to them. She sat in the kitchen, finished her coffee, and got up to see if there was any more in the pot. While she was standing at the stove pouring it, Igor came in quietly.

'Is there any left for me?'

'Yes, I think so.' She peeped into the pot. 'Hmm, enough.'

'I think Boris might make a better nurse than he is a cook,' Igor said. 'The doctor had just returned and he's finding out what will be the best food for her,' he paused and looked at Casey. 'She has lost the child, but there are no complications. She'll be up in a few days.' He poured himself some strong black coffee. 'I went back to the house to collect some clothes for them all while you were looking after them. I don't think we'll have any more trouble from Jean Gallion. I put the fear of God in him.' He smiled faintly. 'He's also going to have a job to get drunk again.'

'Why? How——'

'Doctor Gilles is well respected in the village. He's been telling the innkeeper about what happened—and he is the only doctor for miles, so the innkeeper knows what's best for him, which doesn't include letting Gallion have any more alcohol.'

She closed her eyes. 'What a mess it all is!'

'Yes. But they are safe here now. You had your way after all.'

She stared at him. 'I didn't want it like *that*——'

'I know. But it happened—as it inevitably would have, sooner or later. And perhaps it was best now, while you are here to look after her, who knows?'

While you are here, he said, and the words echoed in Casey's ears as she walked over to the window of the kitchen with her cup of coffee. And soon I'll be going, she thought.

'Jack is late,' Igor observed.

'Jack?' For one absurd moment she wondered who Jack was. 'Oh, yes—he'll be in soon. I'd better get my things moved from my old room to this new one.'

'I will do it for you.'

'There's no need. It won't take me long.'

'As you wish.'

'Igor, is there a camp bed here?'

'A camp bed—I think not. Why?'

'Because it might be better if I slept in the room with Madame Gallion, at least for tonight.'

'But your room adjoins hers—you need only leave the door open.'

'Yes, I know, but I think it's better if she has someone there with her.'

'Then I will find something. There is a small bed somewhere.' He held out his hand. 'Come and help me find it.'

'Let me finish my coffee first.' Did he expect her

to hold his hand? Yet it had been an entirely unconscious gesture on his part, she felt sure, a 'let's go and look together' gesture. Then he touched her arm instead, and ushered her out.

Up the stairs they went, then up again, this time up the spiral staircase towards the top floor. In one of the rooms near the turret, Igor found what he was looking for. 'Will this do for you?' It was small and narrow, more suited to a child.

'Yes, that'll be fine. If we can just take it down——'

'I will get Boris to help.'

'I can. We'll take it now, then I can put the sheets on.' Igor looked at her.

'It will be difficult, down those stairs——'

'I know. But I'm strong. We'll manage.'

He shrugged. 'I know better than to argue with you,' and he bent and lifted the mattress from it and began unscrewing the bolts holding it together. You could have fooled me, Casey thought. And yet had he not changed over the last few hours? Gone was the prickly antagonism that usually entered at some part into any discussion they had. There had been so much to do, and it had all been done swiftly and easily. She looked at him crouching down, looked at his bent head, and was suddenly filled with an overwhelming surge of intense emotion that frightened her. Suddenly, as if he was equally aware of it, he turned his head and looked at her.

'This——' he stood up. 'Casey? What is it? You have gone white.'

She couldn't answer, and he came to her and held her arms. 'Are you not well?'

'I—it's nothing.'

'But yes, tell me, please.' She wanted him to kiss her. She wanted it very much. And that was the second frightening thing. I love Jack, she thought desperately, and this is all wrong. You can only love one man at a time ... 'Casey?' he shook her gently. 'Tell me——'

She shivered. The feeling had passed. Then she smiled. 'Nothing. I suppose I'm tired. When—when we've taken this down, I'll go to bed.'

'Of course. This has been a crowded day for you.' Whether he believed her or not was immaterial. He appeared to, and that was what counted. 'The two children are watching television and the little one is asleep. I will leave the dogs downstairs tonight. If you need anything at all, you must come and wake me, you understand?'

'Yes, I will—I promise.'

'Doctor Gilles will be going soon. Come, I think we had better go and see him, then return for this. You are sure you are well?'

'Yes.'

'Then let us go. We will only be a minute.'

'Of course—I'd forgotten he was here.'

'I know.' He led the way out, and down to the room where Madame Gallion lay.

She looked much better after eating, and was sitting

up in bed, less white-faced than before. Doctor Gilles looked up as they went in.

'Ah, *mademoiselle*,' he said. 'Your patient is ready for you. I have given her a sleeping pill, and I will call in again in the morning.' He looked at Igor. 'A word with you, *m'sieur*, if you please.' The two men went outside, and Casey smiled at the young woman lying in the bed.

'I'll stay in here with you tonight,' she said. 'You'll feel stronger in the morning after a good night's sleep.'

The woman smiled faintly. 'You are so kind,' she murmured. 'So very kind—and M'sieur Igor too. If it were not for him——' her face crumpled.

'Ssh, don't talk,' Casey soothed.

'I must. He is a good man, he has done so much to help, with food and clothes for my children, no one will ever know how much. Are you to be married?'

The question shook Casey. 'Oh no,' she said hastily, 'we share the *château*, that is all.'

'But I saw the way he looked at you, yesterday, and I thought——' she paused, closing her eyes. Casey wondered if she had fallen asleep. She very much wanted to know what Madame Gallion had thought. In fact she couldn't help herself.

'Madame Gallion?' she said gently.

She opened her eyes. 'Please, call me Claire—I saw his look, and it seemed——' again a pause, while Casey waited, hardly daring to breathe. 'It seemed to me that he loved you very much.' With a gentle smile she slipped into sleep, while Casey stood looking down at her, filled with a sensation so dizzying that she wondered she could still stand up. Very quietly, she went and sat down in the chair. For the moment it was all she was capable of doing.

Once, during the night, Claire Gallion woke, crying out, and Casey slipped out of bed and went to her side, but she had fallen asleep again. After waiting a moment to make sure, she padded quietly into the children's room, and checked them. All were fast asleep, each one clutching a toy that Igor had brought from their home. Casey moved the battered teddy that Annette held away from her face, and returned to her room. There she lay quietly for a few minutes, and remembered Claire's words. She hadn't known what she was saying, of course. Sleeping pills could play funny tricks—still, they had shaken Casey at the time. Shortly afterwards, when the doctor had gone, and her bed had been made up, and she had been undressing, she had heard a car and gone to the window, to see Jack getting out of a Rolls-Royce at the front of the *château*, standing waving as it drove away, then walking rather unsteadily to the door. She had gone to bed, very thoughtful.

Two days, that was all they had been here, and already her safe steady world had been turned upside down. She thought this as she lay there, trying to get to sleep again. Everything, in the end, came back to Igor. He was like the centre of a hurricane, the eye round which everything whirled chaotically while he remained steady. He makes trouble for everyone, she thought, and knew immediately that it wasn't strictly true. It wasn't so much that he made trouble as that things happened around him. She searched for the word that eluded her, then remembered it. Catalyst, she thought. That's it, he's a catalyst—someone that changes other people's lives without himself being changed. Perhaps, she thought, I shall tell him in the morning. But by the morning she had forgotten it completely.

It was Sunday, and she could hear church bells in the distance when she woke and looked at her watch. It was nearly seven o'clock. Casey sat up, and saw Claire Gallion watching her. Immediately she went over to her, feeling guilty that she had slept so soundly.

'How do you feel?' she asked her.

'A little better. I am so thirsty——'

'I'll make you coffee. I'll go down now.' Casey picked up her dressing gown from the chair. 'I could do with one myself.' She smiled at Claire. 'I'll not be long, then I'll wash you.' She went out and down the stairs, realising she had forgotten her slippers only when the cold stone struck home. Perhaps I'm getting like him, she thought, and shivered, wondering how he could walk everywhere as he did with no shoes on. The subject of her pondering was in the kitchen when she went in, heating water in the kettle.

'Oh. Good morning,' Casey said. 'I've come down for coffee for Claire and me.'

'Good morning. I'm making it now,' Igor told her. 'Sit down. How is the patient?'

'She seems better. The doctor said she could have a bath today if she wants. Will there be hot water?'

'Yes. We have a heater, and it is already on. Don't leave her alone in the bath.'

'I won't, don't worry.' She sat down at the table. Igor was dressed, if it could be called that, in his jeans. No shirt, no shoes—and he badly needed a shave. She really didn't want to look at him, but it was extremely difficult not to. 'The children need clothes,' she said. 'I'd like to get them some. Where are the nearest clothes shops?'

'Cannes—but you won't get any today. It is Sunday.'

'Yes, I know. But I'll get Jack to run me there to-morrow.'

'Things are expensive there.' He left the coffee pot to stand and pulled up a chair opposite her.

'It doesn't matter.' Didn't he realise how aggressively male he looked? Probably not. He was used to being thus—it was Casey who felt embarrassed by the sheer masculinity of the hard muscular figure opposite her. She cleared her throat. 'I—er—heard Jack come in last night,' she said. Talking about him would help, and she'd be going in a minute anyway.

'Yes? I made him coffee. He had had a pleasant day.' The words held no irony—or none she could detect, but with Igor you couldn't be absolutely sure. 'I told him about our guests, of course.'

'Of course. How did he take it?'

'How would you expect him to?' There was no mistaking the gentle mockery now. Casey felt herself flush.

'I don't know. I'm asking you,' she answered.

He raised an eyebrow. 'He was—surprised. But not too surprised, because'—he paused delicately—'he was, how shall I put it? Rather tired?'

'Do you mean drunk?' she asked bluntly.

Igor looked mildly shocked. Or was he trying not to laugh? Casey stood up. 'I'll pour out the coffee,' she said.

'Let me do it.' It was a mistake. He was too near again. She moved irritably away and heard him laugh. 'No, not drunk. Perhaps a little merry, that is all.' He reached over in front of her and lifted the coffee pot from the stove. 'Ah yes, that is done. You want milk?'

He looked down at her, and Casey at him. She wanted to stroke his cheek—what an absurd thought to have! 'Milk? Er—yes.'

'You slept badly?' He didn't move away. The brown eyes held her.

'No. What makes you say that?' She looked around. 'Where's the milk? I'll get it.' He put the coffee pot down again.

'You seem confused,' he said gently. 'If you're tired you must rest. Boris or I will look after Madame Gallion——'

'I'm not confused at all,' she snapped. 'And I'm not tired. I'm fine—I've never felt better.'

'That is good.' He put his hand beneath her chin, and lifted it slightly. 'Yes, of course, you look very well——'

'Don't——' she croaked.

'Don't touch?'

'Yes, I don't like you always——'

'No, it is very impertinent of me, is it not?' He suddenly caught her hand and lifted it to his face, rubbing her palm over the bristles. Casey snatched her hand away. 'Why did you do that?' she gasped.

'Because you wanted me to. I could see it in your eyes. You thought to yourself, I wonder what it feels like to be kissed by a man when he needs a shave——'

'I didn't! I——' she exclaimed.

'And now you will know,' he said, pulling her to him, and kissing her hard. Then he released her, and he was laughing. Backing away, out of reach, ducking as she lashed out——'Be careful——Casey!'

But it was too late. Her flailing arm had missed him and caught the coffee pot instead. There was a crack, like a pistol shot, a sudden pain as the hot liquid cascaded over her arm—then he moved like lightning, put on the tap and held her arm under the cold gushing water.

'Keep it there,' he said, and held her. He was close behind her, his body against hers, and she couldn't move if she wanted to. His voice came in her ear. 'Casey, forgive me.'

She was shaking. The pain was diminishing, to be replaced by another. She felt the hard length of his body close against hers, and turned, resting her face on his chest. Groaning, he embraced her, their bodies melting together as they stood there quiet and unmoving for what seemed like minutes.

'Do you forgive me?' he whispered. 'I would never hurt you——'

'I know. I didn't see how near it was.' She clung to him tightly, not wanting to move, knowing that what she was doing was utterly wrong, but powerless to do anything about it.

Jack walked in. They didn't even notice him until the heavily sarcastic voice said: 'Well, *well*, how cosy. Can anyone join in?'

Casey whirled round, and Igor said calmly: 'Casey has just scalded her arm.'

'Yes?' Jack walked across the room towards them. 'And I suppose you were making it better?' He gave her a contemptuous glance. 'I'd stand well clear if I were you. I'm not going to miss him this time,' and he swung out his fist at Igor's face. There was nothing she could do—Jack was too mad for that. She saw Igor's arm come up and parry the blow, jolting Jack, who went in closer, punching hard. She didn't want to watch, but she was riveted to the spot, feeling sick, helpless to do anything to stop the mad onslaught. And Igor wasn't hitting back, that was the incredible thing. He defended himself—and she knew with sudden clarity that he didn't want to hurt Jack. Each blow was even more furious. She heard his muttered: 'Fight, damn you, fight!' and found her voice.

'Stop it, Jack, please——' Crying, she tried to pull him away, and went spinning back, to nearly fall, as Jack's arm caught her. Then suddenly it was all over. Igor's hand went up, and Jack staggered and fell, and sat on the floor groaning.

'Oh! Now see what you've done!' Casey burst out, turning on Igor, who stood rubbing his arm.

'*I?* What did you expect me to do? He would not stop. Besides, he hit you.'

'He didn't mean to!' she gasped.

'And I did not mean to hit him.'

'You liar! Get out. Leave me with him. Go on!' her eyes blazed at him. 'Go and see Claire if you want something to do. Tell her I'll be up in a minute——'

'Ach! Women!' he said harshly. 'You are all mad,' and he went out, slamming the door.

'Jack darling, let me help you up——' she began.

'Don't touch me,' he snarled. 'I can get up on my own without your help.' He rubbed his jaw. 'I hope you're satisfied.'

He sat on the chair and glared at her. 'That does it,' he said. 'I'm getting out of here, then you can do what you like.'

'But I don't want you to—please listen. Look at my arm.' She showed him the angry red patch above her wrist. 'After I scalded myself he held me for a minute——'

'Come on,' he said. 'You were practically eating each other. No wonder you didn't want to kiss me the other night. He's a bloody quick worker—I'd like to strangle him——'

It was becoming more like a nightmare with every second. 'You don't understand,' she said. The only trouble was, Casey didn't herself. She had never experienced anything like the intensity of feeling with Jack that she had with Igor. Her own physical reaction to his embrace had been the more disturbing because of that fact. Yet she felt all mixed up inside, despite that. For Jack was the man she was going to marry. And Igor was nothing—or was he? She no longer knew. Jack's next words were even more of a shock, therefore.

He stood up, albeit groggily. 'I'm going,' he said. 'I'll be back for my things later.'

'Going? Going where?' Everything seemed to be slipping away in a dizzying spiral.

'To Lucia's. She'll put me up, until you come to your senses.' He walked towards the door, and when he reached it he turned. 'I told you what he was like when we first arrived. And I was right.'

'What do you mean?'

'Just this, my dear Casey. You don't think he and Lucia are just casual acquaintances, do you?' He laughed. 'God, you're naïve! She was his mistress for two years, until he met someone else—but I'll say this for him. He might discard women like old gloves, but he likes to stay friends with them afterwards—in case they can be useful to him. Especially the wealthy ones.' And he walked out, slamming the door just as Igor had done.

Casey went over to the sink. Running the tap, she plunged her hands under it and began to splash her face. She had never felt so wretched in her life.

Then, very calmly, she filled the kettle to make more coffee. She couldn't leave. Not until Claire was better. But then she would. And she would never come back again.

CHAPTER EIGHT

CASEY avoided Igor for the rest of the day. It was quite easy to do. She busied herself looking after Claire and Annette, while Emil and Marie played in the *château*. It began to rain later in the afternoon, and went quite dark. The doctor called, gave her some ointment for the scald on her arm, and pronounced himself satisfied with Claire's condition. And when Boris knocked at the door later to tell her that dinner was ready, she told him she would eat hers with Claire.

Jack had gone out and not returned. Still numbed by what had happened, Casey was nevertheless so occupied by looking after Claire that it became less painful with each hour that passed to remember. She went over the scene in her mind a dozen times. She deserved her punishment, she knew that. Igor was nothing but a womaniser, and she had so nearly let herself be dazzled by him. But it wouldn't happen again. When she next saw Jack, she would be able to look him in the eye and admit how stupid she had been.

She felt her flesh crawl at the memory of Igor's touch. And she had actually enjoyed it! Shame filled her. She sat on the chair in the bedroom and patiently spooned a mashed-up mixture of bananas and honey into Annette's mouth. It was a revolting-looking concoction, but the baby appeared to be enjoying it, and Casey caught Claire's eyes across the room, and smiled. 'She is very good, isn't she?'

'Yes,' Claire agreed. 'And so are you.'

'I'm glad to help. When I've cleaned her up I'll let you hold her and go and find the children. Boris will have fed them by now. I dare say they're watching television.'

'Ah yes. We do not—did not have one. They will like that.'

Casey scooped up the last of the bananas, wiped Annette's face with the damp flannel that seemed an essential part of the equipment when caring for children, and handed her over to her mother. 'I won't be long,' she said.

She ran down the stairs and went into the room that had the television in. The children were there, but they weren't watching it. Emil and Marie were playing cards with Igor. For a moment Casey stood just inside the doorway, then Igor looked up.

'You want the children?' he asked.

'Yes. It's nearly bedtime.' She waited.

'We have almost finished this game, then they'll come.' He looked down again at the table. His glance had been entirely impersonal; he spoke as though she were a stranger. He knows, she thought. Somehow, he knows. The rain lashed down outside, and it matched her mood perfectly. There was even a faint coolness in the air.

'Okay.' He picked up the cards, and said to the children: 'Off you go to bed.' They stood up obediently, and he said to Casey: 'Before *you* go, I want a word with you.'

She still stood by the door as the children came towards her. 'I don't think there's anything to say,' she answered.

'Yes, there is.' He rose to his feet and followed them. '*Allez, vite!*' They scampered out, and he closed the door even as Casey went to go after them.

'Where is Jack?' he asked.

'Don't you know?'

'I would not be asking if I did. The car has gone.'

'He told me he was going to stay at Lucia's. He said he'd come back for his things later. He doesn't like it here.' She looked at him coolly.

'I see.' Everything was suddenly very silent, except for the lashing rain outside, and the air crackled with tension. 'How is your arm?'

'Better. Is that all you wanted to say? I want to get the children to bed.'

'No. Why have you been avoiding me all day?'

'I didn't think you'd notice!' she answered.

'But I did. You make things very obvious—and your eyes are cold. I can feel the icicles from here.'

'How perceptive of you!' she snapped.

His own eyes narrowed. 'Perhaps you had better go. I can see you are in no mood for talking to me.'

'You're quite right. If you'll let me open the door——'

He opened it for her, and she walked out. Then she heard it close quietly behind her. She ran quickly up the stairs, and into the bedroom.

It was mid-morning the next day before Casey encountered Igor. She had gone down to the kitchen to make coffee for herself and Claire, and Boris was there preparing lunch. She wondered briefly if he was aware of the atmosphere, but if he was, he gave no sign of it. As unfailingly courteous as ever, he smiled gently at her.

'Mr Borodinov is outside with the children and the dogs,' he told her. 'He asked me to tell you, when you came down, that he will take you to the shops if you wish.'

She had forgotten about the clothes, and stared blankly at him for a moment before remembering. 'Oh, yes, of course. After lunch, perhaps. But how? Does he have a car?' She hadn't seen one.

He smiled. 'Ah yes, in the garage. Shall I tell him or will you?'

'You're busy. I came to make coffee——'

'Then I will make it for you. When you come back it will be ready.'

Casey went out, along the corridor, and down the front steps. She could hear Marie's voice, and one of the dogs barking, from behind the greenhouse, and crossed the grass towards the sound, to see them all busily engaged in planting seeds. Igor looked up, then straightened.

'Boris said you would take us to the shops,' she said. 'Will after lunch be all right?'

'Perfectly. Boris will look after Madame Gallion while we are away.' He stared coolly at her. 'Is that all you came out to say?'

She felt herself flushing. 'Yes.'

'Good.' He bent to his task again. Casey turned and walked back. It certainly makes things easier, she thought—in one way. Yet she felt wretched. His displeasure was a potent thing, as strong as he himself, and as disturbing—in a different way—as his other behaviour.

She carried the coffee upstairs and heard a car draw up outside. Giving Claire hers, she went to the window to see Jack getting out of his car. With him was Lucia and another woman. She saw them go inside, and turned away from the window, her heart beating faster.

'Here, let me put Anette in her cot while you drink your coffee,' she said, putting her own cup down. She lifted the sleeping child from beside her mother and put her in the cot she had brought into the room. It was a huge laundry basket that Igor had found and cleaned the previous day. Nailed firmly to a plain wood table, it was as safe as any modern cot, and as comfortable, lined with blankets. Casey began talking to Claire, telling her what Marie and Emil were doing, firmly putting out of her head any thoughts of Jack. She could hear their voices, the women's laughter, their footsteps as they climbed the stairs.

Then the voices faded, and she heard them overhead, but very faintly. She bit her lip.

'Is anything the matter?'

Casey laughed. 'No, nothing. I was just thinking, that's all. The doctor says you may get up tomorrow —if you feel well enough. And this afternoon, with your permission, I would like to take the children into Cannes.'

'That would be nice for them. But why?'

'Would you let me buy them some clothes—please?'

Claire's eyes clouded, then filled with tears. 'Oh, what have I said?' asked Casey anxiously.

'No, you must not. How can I repay——'

'Oh, but it's nothing. I don't want you to——'

'But he—M'sieur Igor has done so much—and now you——'

And it was at that moment that Casey had the brilliant idea. She wondered why it had never occurred to her before. It was so beautifully simple, and undoubtedly right.

'Claire,' she said, 'listen to me. I know how you feel—I would be just the same as you. But there is a way you might be able to help. He—Igor—is hoping one day to open this *château* as an hotel.'

Claire looked at her uncomprehendingly. 'Don't you see? He'll need staff—you could live here, and work. Then you'd be independent.'

The woman's eyes brightened. 'I can clean, and I can cook—when I get the food—I will do anything.'

She laughed. It was the first time Casey had ever seen her laugh, and it did her good to hear it. 'Oh yes, that is good.'

'So will you let me buy them some clothes? And one day you can pay me back.' Which was a lie, but in a good cause.

'I would be so pleased. They need so many things——' Claire stopped, horrified. 'I didn't mean——'

'No, I know you didn't. We'll just get them enough for now. Drink your coffee and I'll take the cups down.' She could hear the voices again, coming down, then receding, and she went to the window. She saw them come out. Then she saw Igor. He was walking across the grass towards them as casually as if nothing had ever happened. She saw Lucia turn away from Jack, who was engaged in putting his case and some rolled-up blueprints in the boot, and go over to Igor. Transfixed, she watched them talking together on the grass, saw Jack slam the boot lid shut and get in the car, then the other woman wandered over to Lucia and shook hands with Igor. 'I don't believe it,' she thought, and didn't realise she had spoken aloud until Claire said:

'*Pardon?*'

'Oh, nothing. Just some friends of Igor's talking.' It was so casual, as if they were all good friends—which was what, apparently, they were. They live differently, she thought dully. It's like being in another world. And he's part of it. Changing partners—discarding lovers—staying friends. And who was the other woman? She suddenly didn't want to watch, and turned away from the window. 'Yes, well, I'll take these down.' She fled with the cups.

Afterwards she ate lunch in the bedroom with Claire, and then changed into cool white slacks and blue blouse and sandals. Taking the plates, she said:

'Is there anything you need from the shops?'

'Nothing, thank you.'

'Then I'll go. Boris will be up to see if you need anything. *Au révoir.*'

'*Au revoir*, Casey.'

Igor was in the kitchen with Boris and the children. He glanced at her as she went in, and the hardness was back in his eyes. 'We are ready if you are,' he said.

'Yes, I'm ready.' She had her purse in her bag, and the equivalent of sixty pounds in french francs. It would be enough, she hoped, for all she wanted.

'I will bring the car to the front,' he said, and went out.

'Come on, children.' To Boris she added: 'You'll look after Madame Gallion?'

'Yes, I shall go up now. Have a pleasant trip.'

'Thank you.' She doubted it, but there was no alternative.

Igor sat in a Citroën shooting brake at the front entrance, engine throbbing. Casey sat the two children in the back and got in herself, then they were off. He spoke to the children on their journey, but not to

Casey. Which suits me, she thought, but it didn't make her feel any better. Down the track, to the wider road, then on to the main route into Cannes, and he drove fast, but well. Marie chattered to her brother in the back, pointing out familiar landmarks, exclaiming over the sea, laughing as they overtook other vehicles.

Igor's hands were strong on the wheel, and he took the bends in the road casually, the powerful engine doing his bidding, the miles being eaten up inexorably. And still he did not speak to her. Casey began to feel restless, irritated, though she knew not why.

'Are you going to keep silent all day?' she asked.

He took his eyes briefly from the road to glance at her. 'There is nothing to say—you told me that,' he answered.

'Then for their sake you might make the effort,' she said.

'I will, when we arrive. Until then, I prefer to concentrate on driving.'

She drew in her breath. So be it. He had changed, and that was that. She wished she had never come. It had been a mistake. Her engagement was virtually in ruins, she herself was in turmoil, Jack had left her, and Igor, the dark Russian with whom she shared a *château*, was once more the man she had glimpsed in those first few moments of meeting. And yet nothing would ever be the same again.

'Fine. That suits me fine,' she nodded coolly, and looked away out of her window to the breathtaking view on her right. The sea glittered in the afternoon sun and far ahead of her in the distance, she could see the white buildings rising from the harbour at Cannes, and the boats bobbing in the water. It could have been so different, with anyone else, or with him as he could be—it could have been enjoyable. The sea became blurred, and she blinked furiously. There would be no tears. I'm finished crying over men, she thought, and two in particular. You're not worth it. And when Marie asked her a question about where they were going, she was able to answer her perfectly calmly. She was even able to smile.

She discovered that the two children had never been to Cannes before. The pleasure in their eyes—particularly Emil's—was a joy to see. When Igor had parked the car and they were walking round the cluster of busy shops it seemed natural that Emil should hold Casey's hand, and Marie Igor's. They walked in front, and Marie was practically hopping in her excitement. 'Oh, look! Look at that! Look, Emil!' she would exclaim, turning her head to make sure Emil heard. And Casey thought, I'll bet anyone seeing us thinks we're an old married couple out for the day with our children—an oddly disturbing thought to have.

True to his word, Igor spoke to Casey as though nothing was amiss.

'There is no point in visiting any shops on the front,' he said. 'The prices are ridiculous. The back streets are where we'll find clothes for the children.'

'I'll be guided by you,' she agreed. So he led them in a confusing maze of streets, with busy cafés and restaurants and boutiques and antique shops, until he found what he was looking for. The next hour passed busily, with the children trying on clothes, and Casey nodding or shaking her head, until at last two carrier bags were full. They had underclothes, socks, two dresses for Marie, two pairs of shorts and shirts for Emil and clothes for the baby. These she paid for, Igor picked them up, and started to lead them out of the shop. Casey turned back to the proprietress.

'*Madame*,' she said, 'that blue cotton dress in the window—do you happen to have one in a size smaller than I would take?'

The woman stood back, pursed her lips. '*Mais certainement, madame. Un moment.*' She vanished behind the counter and emerged triumphant with a blue dress. '*Voilà!*' Casey paid her, the dress was slipped into a bag, and out she went to join the others. She would manage to persuade Claire to accept it somehow.

'You want to walk down to the harbour and see the yachts?' asked Igor.

'Oh *yes!* Can we?' Marie jumped up and down in excitement, and Emil nodded, eyes bright.

'Come on, then.' Igor led the way, Casey followed with Emil, and the sun beat down on them. It would have been a wonderful day, she thought, if only ...

But the day was not yet over.

It was crowded with tourists down by the boats, and they walked slowly along, eating ice creams, the children's eyes like saucers, Igor laughing with them, the atmosphere beginning to relax, when——

'Casey! By all that's marvellous! Casey—yoo-hoo!' She turned to see a bikini-clad figure waving madly from a sleek blue yacht bobbing in the water. Igor stopped, the children stopped, momentarily silenced, and Casey, slipping her hand out of Emil's, walked back—with strange reluctance—to greet the girl waiting.

'Hello, Kim! What on earth are you doing here?'

'Would you believe I'm working?' Kim's blue eyes danced with laughter. A statuesque six-footer, who was a busy and successful model, she had been at school with Casey, and they met occasionally for lunch, or at parties in London.

'You call this working?' Casey laughed, well aware that several yards away three silent figures watched her.

'It's a modelling assignment, ducky, honest. Up at seven, draping myself against palm trees dressed in dinky little suits—you know the drill—and I met this gorgeous Italian millionaire'—she lowered her voice —'who's flown off to Milan on business, so he's left me in charge of the boat for the day. I'm having a party later. Why don't you come?' Then she noticed Igor. 'My God, *who's* that sexy hunk?' Casey hoped desperately that Kim's voice hadn't carried. The noise of the passing traffic was tremendous, fortunately. 'And where's Jack—you know, your betrothed?'

It would take a day to tell. 'Er—Jack's visiting friends—and *that* is a Russian who happens to be—er —co-owner of a *château* with me.' The story sounded implausible to Casey's ears, even as she said it, and Kim laughed delightedly.

'You're pulling my leg!'

'No, honestly.'

'And the kids? His?'

'No. He's not married. They belong to—er—friends of his. We brought them in to buy them some clothes. Look, I must dash, Kim——'

'Come later, then. About nine. There'll be a crowd here, and Giorgio should be back—and bring *him*.' She smiled and waved at Igor, who smiled and nodded back, politely enough, then spoke to the children.

'Mmm,' said Kim. 'You did say Jack was here too?' Casey could almost hear the wheels turning in Kim's head.

'Oh yes.' At least it was the truth—in a way. 'I'm not sure I'll be able to make the party,' she said, 'but if I don't, we'll get together when you're back in London——'

'Of course we will. Try anyway.' Kim smiled knowingly. 'Though I don't blame you——'

'No. Must go. 'Bye, Kim, lovely to see you.' She walked away to join the others, and when she reached them, looked back and waved. Kim was standing there watching. She lifted her hand in a little salute.

'A friend of yours?' Igor asked politely.

'Yes. A model. She's invited us to a party on the yacht tonight.'

'Really? How kind of her.' Then he turned and spoke to the children.

All right, damn you, thought Casey. You make yourself perfectly clear. Even his back was eloquent, as he walked on. I don't think I want to know your friends, it seemed to say. She pulled out her tongue at him, and it made her feel better.

Then they saw the ferry. The sign said *'Ile des Lérins,'* and the motor chugged as the people climbed aboard the flat craft—and Igor said: 'Do you want to go to an island?' Not to Casey, to the children. The response was immediate.

'Yes. Oh yes!' said Marie.

'Come on, then.' He walked down the slope and Casey followed. They had never been on a boat before, she found out, as the ferry left the harbour and chugged out towards the tree-covered island a short distance away. As they sped through the green water, a canopy overhead protecting them from the sun, Casey thought about Jack. He should have been here with her, not Igor—and it would have been so enjoyable—then she paused in her thought. But he wouldn't have suggested this. It would have been straight to the shops, buy the clothes, and back to the *château*. For children bored him, as he freely admitted. He never knew what to say to them. And with Marie and Emil he'd be lost anyway because he didn't speak French. She sighed a little sigh. They were enjoying themselves tremendously, that was obvious.

They enjoyed themselves even more when they had landed on the Ile Ste Marguerite and Igor led them down to a beach and sat down on the sand, putting the parcels of clothes in the shade. Casey, after a moment's hesitation, sat down too, and the children ran off, scampering joyously across the golden sand, after kicking off their shoes. And so they were alone, or virtually so.

He looked at her. 'You wish to go to this party to-night?'

'Of course not! I have to look after Claire and the children.'

'Boris and I can manage. You may have the car. You can drive?'

'Yes, but I don't want——'

'But she is your friend. It is nice to visit friends, is it not?'

'*Yes,* but I'm not mad about parties——'

'I would have thought you were.' The hard brown eyes mocked her.

'Then you're wrong. Do you? You can go if you want——'

'They are not my friends, are they?'

'Perhaps you'd let me finish a sentence sometimes!' she snapped. 'Instead of interrupting.' She stopped. Igor remained silent. Casey sighed. She might as well face the fact that she could do no right. If he wasn't being aggressive, or completely withdrawn, he was mocking her, and she didn't know which was worse. 'I don't want to go out tonight to Kim's party,' she said slowly. 'Do I make myself clear?'

'Perfectly.' He plucked a piece of long grass from the bank against which he rested, and began to chew it. 'Because Jack would not be with you?'

'That has nothing to do with it.'

'No? But it is better to have an escort, no?'

'It all depends what kind of party it is. I don't know the kind *you* go to,' and she smiled innocently. 'But I can imagine.' He didn't have the monopoly on insults.

He laughed. 'Tell me what you imagine.'

'No, I'd rather not.' She looked away and along the beach to see the children paddling, kicking up water at each other, faces laughing. 'I'm glad they're enjoying themselves,' she added.

'Are you not?'

'With you?' she laughed. 'What do you think?' She turned to face him. 'You've ruined my engagement, behaved outrageously, and you dare to ask if I'm enjoying myself? I wish I'd never come here.'

'To *here*—or to the *château*?'

'Both,' she answered.

'Nobody is keeping you there. You can always leave.'

'I intend to as soon as I can, don't worry.'

Igor flung the grass away from him. 'And have you decided what you will do about my suggestion?'

'I've thought about it, yes.'

'And?'

'I haven't made up my mind.' She smiled slowly. 'When I do, you'll know.'

'You don't have to sell to me. You could always go halves in the hotel——'

'With you as my partner?' She stared at him, disbelievingly.

'It has been done before.' He carefully selected another piece of grass.

'You're mad to even suggest it!' she breathed.

'Am I? I think not. I am no more mad than you are. And you, under that childish exterior, I think you have a shrewd brain.'

'Under my childish exterior! My goodness, that's good, coming from you!' She glared angrily at him.

'You have not yet grown up.' He shrugged. 'How old are you? Twenty—twenty-one?'

'I'm twenty-three. Not that it's any of your business,' she breathed.

'But you care, about people—and animals,' he went on, as if she hadn't spoken. 'There is hope for you. Jack, he is different——'

'We'll leave him out of it. You've done enough——'

'He cares about nothing except himself.'

'I said——'

'You know that already. You must know that. He is better gone. He and Lucia are two of a kind.'

'Oh yes! And you'd know that, wouldn't you?' she stormed. 'You know *her* very well——'

'Ah, so *that* is it.' He gave a satisfied sigh. 'There *is* something. What did Jack tell you?'

'Can't you imagine?' Furious, shaking, knowing at last where all his questions had been leading, Casey stared at him, fists clenched, breathing hard.

'No, I cannot. But I have known that you were changed since that morning——'

'And you can't imagine why? You must be stupid——' He caught her wrist in a grip of steel.

'Not stupid, but very curious. Tell me.' The fingers tightened round her wrist.

'Let *go*!'

'When you say what is eating away at you——'

'Nothing's eating away at *me*! I don't care what you are—but you're not going to——' She winced.

'Tell me.'

'All right, you brute. You and Lucia were lovers—I know that—and you discard women——'

He let go of her wrist and rolled away, laughing. Casey launched herself on him. 'Don't you dare laugh! You *beast*—you——' Fists pummelling at his chest, then suddenly she was helpless as he caught her wrists and held her. His face had gone serious.

'Is that what he told you?'

'Yes.' She lay back and looked up at him, leaning over her. 'Yes—yes—*yes*!'

'Then one of them is lying. And I think I know which one.' He pulled her up to her feet and they stood facing each other. 'She has never been my mistress. Never.'

'I don't believe you.'

'I tell you the truth.' She looked in his eyes and saw what was in them, and a cold wave rushed over her.

'Then why——?' she began quietly, subdued. 'Why would she——'

'I don't know. You must understand the workings of a woman's mind better than I. Oh, I was aware that she was interested. I am not so blind—but she does not—never has—appealed to me in that way.'

'She's a very attractive woman. Are you trying to tell me——'

'I am not *trying* to tell you, I *am* telling you. I do not go around making love to every woman I see.'

'But Jack said——'

'I care not for what Jack said!' he retorted bluntly. 'He does not know me at all. I know what he thinks——' he gave her a grim smile. 'He made that obvious. As perhaps,' he allowed, 'I made clear what I thought of him. And he had the right to be angry when he came into the kitchen and saw us——'

'Please, I don't want to go over that——' Casey began, utterly confused.

'It is necessary, because he knew then what I did not. I did not fight him back, I only defended myself——'

'You knocked him flying!'

'Only because he struck you——'

'But that was——' she stopped. What had he just said? 'What do you mean, he knew then what you didn't?'

A sudden frightened shriek came from Marie, and Igor turned, and sprinted away towards them. But the four words he said, just before he started to run, were plain enough. 'That I want *you*.'

CHAPTER NINE

Marie had fallen in the water. Her clothes were drenched, but she was more frightened than hurt, and when Igor reached her she was scrambling out, helped by Emil, and ran into Igor's arms.

'I fell, I fell!' she babbled.

'Never mind,' he soothed. 'You have some new clothes to put on. See? I think you did it on purpose.' Casey had followed, and she took Emil's hand as they walked back to where they had been sitting. She was too shaken to think clearly, almost glad of the diversion which had cut short their conversation.

Igor put Marie down, then turned to Emil. 'Come with me while Casey changes your sister,' he said, and the two of them walked away to scramble up the rocks to the road.

'Take your dress off, Marie,' Casey told her, 'and I'll find you your new one. Which would you like, the blue or the pink?'

Marie was beginning to enjoy the fuss. 'Mmm, the blue, please.' She tugged off her soaking wet dress and flung it on the sand.

'Did you swallow any water?' Casey asked.

'No. I slipped on some seaweed—I was frightened.'

'Of course you were,' Casey soothed. 'Come on now, get this on. Oh my, that looks nice!' She smiled at the girl, who preened herself and pirouetted round. 'Look, you might as well put on some dry pants.' She found a pair with glorious pink flowers, and Marie changed into them. Casey bundled up the wet dress and pants, transferred Claire's dress to one of the other bags, and put the wet clothes in the plastic bag.

'Feel better?' she said.

'Yes.' Marie smiled. 'Thank you for these.'

'You're welcome.' A clinking of glass was heard, and Igor and Emil reappeared carrying three bottles, straws, and plastic cups. They scrambled down onto the beach and sat down.

'Coke for you, Marie—and for you, Emil,' Igor said. 'And here, have a straw each.' He looked at Casey, and handed her a plastic cup. 'Wine?' he asked.

'Please.' She watched him pour out two cupfuls. 'I thought you didn't drink,' she said.

He shrugged. 'A little wine occasionally.' He lifted his cup. '*Na zdorovye.*'

'Cheers.' They drank. It was a dry white wine, and she hadn't realised how thirsty she was. The children sat sipping their Coca-cola through straws, and Casey looked at Igor. Perhaps she had imagined what he had said. After all, he had been running away from her at the time. She could so easily have mis-heard ...

'Soon we must leave.' He spoke in French for the benefit of the children, whose faces fell.

'Please—another paddle, with you,' Marie begged.

He shrugged. 'Perhaps when you have finished your drink.' He lifted the bottle. 'More, Casey?'

'A little.'

'Oh no, we must finish the bottle. Come, your cup.' He filled it again, then his own. She drank it, and it was beginning to have the most pleasant effect on her, going right down to her toes, making her head feel very light.

'And so—there, it is all gone.' She realised her cup was now filled again, looked dazedly at it, then giggled.

'Why not?' She drank it all, then stood up. 'Let's all go for a paddle.' She kicked off her sandals and ran into the water. The children followed, and then Igor. It was sheer bliss, thought Casey, as she lifted her face to the sun. The warm water shushing round her feet, the constant chirrup of the cicadas in the eucalyptus trees behind them, the warmth—sheer bliss. She would not have changed places with anyone just then. What did anything else matter? Now, this moment, was all that counted. She heaved a deep sigh of contentment, and Igor, ahead of her, turned and looked at her. He was ever so slightly blurred round the edges. Even his voice sounded different.

'You're drunk,' he said.

'No, I'm not.' She blinked at him.

He turned away, but she saw his smile. 'I'm not,' she repeated, in case he hadn't heard. 'I'm perfectly sh-sober.' She had slight difficulty with the last word, so said it again. 'Sober.'

'Yes, of course you are.'

She suddenly decided she had had enough paddling, and walked out to sit down on the beach. Then she lay back and closed her eyes, feeling the hot sun blazing on her face. She wasn't sure if he had been laughing at her, but it was quite unimportant. They would be going back to the *château* soon, and she didn't really want to go, she wanted to stay there and just lie in the sun, and get brown . . .

Something tickled her nose, and she opened her eyes to see Igor holding a piece of grass stroking it on her face. She sat up.

'Where are the children?'

'Gone to take the bottles back to the café. You've been asleep.'

'I haven't, have I?'

'Yes.' He sat down beside her, and looked at her. 'If this is what a little wine does for you, it's better you do not go to the party tonight.'

She stifled a yawn. 'I'm not going anyway. I thought we'd been over that——' and then it all came back to her. All of it. She looked at him, the knowledge in her eyes. 'I——' she caught her breath, and looked away lest he saw.

'I? What were you going to say?'

'Nothing. Hadn't we better be leaving?'

'When they get back, yes.' Casey studied her sand-covered toes, and began to brush away the golden grains. 'Do I frighten you so much?' Igor asked softly.

'I don't know what you mean——'

'You do not look at me when you speak. Because you think I see what you try to hide.'

She looked up then. 'Perhaps you do, I don't know.'

'Sometimes I do, yes. Because—you know why.'

'Because you're a mind-reader?' she suggested flippantly. 'You could earn a lot of money——'

'No, not that. I told you once why.'

'And I've forgotten. And in any case I don't want to talk about——'

'So you do remember what I said? That we have known each other——' she scrambled to her feet and turned away.

'I'm not going to listen. I'm going to look for the children——'

'You can't run away from yourself.'

She whirled round on him. 'I'm not trying to,' she answered. 'But I can't think straight with you. Oh!' she put her hand to her head.

He began to laugh, not cruelly, but gently. 'Poor Casey! Too much sun and wine.' He took her arm. 'See, there they are in the distance. Put your sandals on, and we will go. There is a ferry in ten minutes.'

He picked up all the bags, including her shoulder bag, while Casey hopped about trying to put her sandals on. 'Here,' he caught her arm. 'Lean on me.'

His touch was fire, but short of snatching her hand away there was nothing she could do about it. 'Thanks,' she said, and they began scrambling up the rocks to where the children waited.

Fifteen minutes later they were speeding back over the water to Cannes.

It had apparently all been happening while they were away. When they reached the *château*, the doctor had been, Boris told them, and said that Claire might get up. When Casey went into the bedroom, it was to see her dressed, sitting in a large easy chair by the window, and reading a book.

'You look fine,' Casey said delightedly. She pulled out the clothes she had bought for the children, and showed them to her—then, with a little flourish, brought out the dress and held it up. 'I couldn't resist this,' she said. 'Please try it on.'

Claire looked at the blue cotton, her cheeks going pink. 'For me?' she whispered.

'Don't be offended. It was so pretty. I'd like you to have it.'

'Oh, thank you. Of course I'm not offended.' She held Casey's hand. 'Help me up, please. I may try it now?'

'Yes. The children will be up in a minute. They're just telling Boris all about their day out. They'll sleep well tonight.'

It fitted perfectly, although it was rather long, and Claire looked much younger, and quite different. She stared at herself in the mirror. 'What can I say?' she said.

'Nothing. Here are your children. Come in.' Casey left them to tell their mother all about their day out, and went downstairs to the kitchen.

Igor and Boris were talking quietly when she went in, then stopped. 'Your meal is ready,' Boris told her. 'You will eat here, or upstairs?'

'Here. Then I'll take up Claire's,' she said.

'No need. She has eaten. So has the little one.' He smiled. 'I do quite well when you are out, no?'

'You do wonderfully well,' Casey laughed. She felt like hugging him. In fact she felt *good*. She wasn't sure why, but the main thing was that she did. And it showed in her face. It glowed with the sun, and her eyes sparkled—and Igor watched her and said:

'An evening out will do you good.'

'The party?' She looked briefly at Boris. 'But I don't want to—and in any case, I wouldn't dream of driving for the first time at night in a strange place.'

'No problem. I will take you.'

She didn't know whether he meant he would take her and drop her there, or go with her. She looked at him, puzzled, and realised what he and Boris had been talking about when Boris said:

'Madame Gallion is much better, and the children are no trouble. I am happy to mind them.'

'You have been working hard here,' added Igor. 'You need a change.' Was it a conspiracy? And yet there came a stirring of excitement within her. She managed to suppress it, and said doubtfully: 'Well —I——'

'You have a long dress?'

'I brought one, yes.' She looked at them both. 'Why not?' After all that had happened, it would make little difference. She sighed. Perhaps it would even do her good. She began to plan ahead. It was seven now, that gave her an hour to sort out the small tasks she had to do, and half an hour to get ready ... There was no need to stay late at the party. An hour or two would be nice. Only one thing puzzled her, and that was why Igor should be so interested in their going. And she would ask him that question when they were on their way. Whether she got a straight answer or not was another matter ...

'Why did you offer to take me?' she asked him, as they sped down the drive.

'Why?' he seemed to ponder the question. 'It seemed a good idea. After all our misunderstandings'—he shrugged—'I thought it was the least I could do.'

'I don't understand you.'

He laughed. 'Good. Leave it like that. You may enjoy the evening better, who knows?'

It was so very different from their morning's journey when he had been like a cool hard stranger. He was relaxed—and he looked completely different, that was the more startling thing. Usually so casual —bordering on unkempt—he was a changed man. Slim-fitting black trousers, a white open-necked shirt, clean-shaven, and his hair still damp from washing, he was devastatingly attractive. And Casey had never seen him in socks and shoes before. She hadn't even thought he possessed any. The car's headlights cut a swathe through the darkness, and the excitement stirred in her again.

'Thank you for taking me,' she said. 'I suppose I did need a night out.'

'And me. I have not been out since—no, I cannot even remember when.' He glanced briefly at her. 'How long do you want to stay?'

'Not too late. Twelve?'

He shrugged. 'Yes, of course. It is for you to decide.'

She leaned back in her seat. 'One thing—please don't let me drink too much.'

He laughed. 'I do not think you will. And you need not worry about me. I shall have only wine— and not much of that.'

Casey closed her eyes, thinking of Jack. It should have been him taking her, and it would have been like old times. But perhaps they would never return. Perhaps it was all over. She would know soon enough. Life would go on, even so.

'Sleepy?'

'No. Thinking.' She opened her eyes.

'About Jack?'

'How did you know?'

'You gave a little sigh. I always know.'

'Then I must remember not to.' She touched her engagement ring. That was real enough anyway.

She looked out over the sheer drop on her right, to the sea. It was so very different at night, the sky a deep velvety blue, glittering with stars, and a high cool moon floating along, keeping—it seemed—the same speed as they. He drove faster than he had during the day, and the cars swished past them on their left, going in the opposite direction, head-lights blazing, occasionally with horns blaring. She felt as if she were in a dream. Nothing seemed real any more. She reached up and smoothed back her hair, and he said:

'You look very beautiful tonight, Casey.'

'Do I? Thank you.' She smiled softly in the dark.

'Jack is a fool to have left.'

'Can we——' her voice felt strained. 'Can we avoid the subject of Jack, and anything else—just for tonight?'

'To keep the peace? That is sensible. I promise I will not mention him again this evening. Is there anything else you wish me not to talk about?'

'The list is endless,' she murmured dryly, more to herself than him, but he heard anyway, and chuckled richly.

'Then let us think instead of the subjects that are not forbidden.' There was a brief pause. 'Hmm, we can talk about the weather—that is a favourite topic of conversation with you English, I believe—and animals, I suppose—wild geese in particular—and—um, yes, there does not seem to be much else.'

The glittering lights of Cannes were spread along ahead of them like a diamond necklace in the night. 'We can talk about your ideas for an hotel,' she murmured.

'We can?' he looked startled. 'Surely that is another awkward subject?'

'Not any more. I took it upon myself to mention it to Claire. I was sure you wouldn't mind. And you will need staff.'

'Of course. A good idea. And what else have you thought about it?'

'It's intriguing. The *château* would be used—it's hardly being touched at the moment. A lot of people would like the idea of sleeping in a genuine castle— I think it has great possibilities.'

'So at last we find something to agree on. I find that astounding.'

'There's no need to be sarcastic!'

'Did you think I was?'

'If you must know—yes.'

He laughed. 'Perhaps I was. Very well, I'll be serious. A lot of work is needed. The bathrooms, as you have seen for yourself, are ancient. They will have to be modernised, as will some of the rooms upstairs. But I will keep the essential character of the place, naturally. The tapestry room, the room with the stained glass windows, all are part of its personality. Then I will have to extend the vegetable garden so that we will be self-sufficient regarding most of the food. But it can be done. And I will do it.'

Casey listened to him, caught by the sheer enthusiasm in his voice, fascinated by the picture he painted. And it was what her uncle would have wished.

'Yes,' she said slowly, 'I think you will.'

They were nearly there, and ahead of them lay the harbour. 'I will have to park where I can,' Igor said, 'and we will walk the rest of the way.'

He hadn't asked the most obvious question of her, and Casey sensed he did not intend to. She didn't want him to, because she had still not decided what her answer would be. To sell, or not to sell. A simple enough question—and yet not. But there was time. Not much, but a few days would be all she needed. For in her mind she knew she could not stay at the Château Fleuron for much longer. Already her happy ordered existence had been sent topsy-turvy by this dark unpredictable man by her side. For her own sake, her own peace of mind, she must get away before it was too late.

She suddenly knew, as Igor locked the car in the well lit parking space he had found, that she didn't really want to go to the party after all. It had been a mistake to come. She would know nobody, except Kim, who as a busy hostess could hardly be expected to say more than a quick 'hi' in passing.

'I don't want to go,' she told Igor. 'I've changed my mind.'

'But we are here now,' he pointed out. He took

163

her arm to guide her over the busy road full of maniac drivers, and pointed at the lights in the harbour. Bobbing lights from well lit yachts and smaller craft. 'Listen—do you not hear the music?' A pop song throbbed in the warm air, and they went nearer, and the music grew louder, even above the blare of the traffic, and he kept hold of her arm. 'You said yourself we will not stay long, so relax.'

She stopped. 'But I——'

'Yes?' He looked down at her, face solicitous, faintly smiling.

'You talked me into it,' she went on lamely.

'Only because you needed to get away from everything for a while. You have taken on a big responsibility, looking after three children and their mother. The least I could do to repay you was to bring you here. So——' his hand tightened on her elbow, 'you will smile and tell yourself what fun you are going to have. And that is an order.'

The boat rocked with noise, and already it was crowded. It was a fair sized yacht, brightly lit, and as they walked down the gangplank, Kim detached herself from a group of laughing people and came over to them, hands out in welcome. She kissed Casey warmly. 'You made it! Come and join this mad lot in here—my God, I think everyone in Cannes has arrived and brought a friend.' She reached up and gave Igor a smacking kiss.

'Kim, Igor—Igor, Kim,' said Casey.

'Umm, yes—super to have you aboard. Come on in and I'll try and introduce you.' She pushed her way through the crowded deck, holding Casey's hand tightly, shouted a few names, then darted off to greet newcomers. 'Won't be long, darlings.' They didn't see her again. A white-coated waiter handed them drinks, and they stood wedged inside the doorway of the main saloon and Casey looked at Igor, who, towering as he did head and shoulders above most of the men there, was looking round him interestedly. There was a lot to see. Casey felt distinctly old-fashioned in the flame chiffon dress that swirled round her. She had thought it rather low-necked. The dresses that some of the other women wore—or nearly wore—left little to the imagination. Igor started up a conversation with a striking redhead who had made a beeline for him, then Casey turned at a touch on her arm and looked to see a large crew-cut American sailor grinning at her. 'Dance, honey?' he said in a Texas drawl.

'Is it possible?' She looked round bemused.

'On deck. Follow me.' He took her hand and pushed his way through the close-packed bodies on to the deck outside, where several couples moved together in a dreamy waltz—which had the virtue of being a little quieter than the pop music.

'Hey, this is some boat, hey?' The Texan grinned down at her as he held her tightly. 'These friends of yours?'

'Well, one is,' she admitted. 'And you?'

'Nope, I was just passing, and someone hauled me aboard. Name's Chuck, by the way.'

'Casey.'

'Hi, Casey. You alone?'

'No, I'm with a friend.'

'Yeah, just my luck. He bigger than me?'

She laughed. 'A bit.' His accent was as amusing as anything else about him, and that he appeared to be doing a samba to the waltz music mattered not at all. He kept her laughing with a constant stream of smooth patter, wove in and out along the crowded deck and pushed her into a dark corner.

'Phew, that's better. Let's sit and talk awhile. You want a drink?'

'I had one, but I put it down to dance with you,' she answered.

'Okay, watch this. Stay right there.' He vanished, returning less than a minute later with two filled glasses. 'How's that for speed? Now tell me all about yourself, Casey.'

'It would take too long,' she murmured. 'Anyway, it's rather bad manners to leave my escort—we've only just arrived——'

'He the big guy talking to the redhead?'

'Yes.'

'They're dancing, honey. Like they was *glued* together.' Casey peeped round from her hidden seat, and saw Igor, the redheaded girl firmly wrapped round him as he steered a course in the limited deck space. A sudden completely irrational shaft of jealousy pierced her. She leant back, took a good swallow of the champagne, and said:

'I want to dance too, Chuck—you're such a good dancer.'

'I am?' he looked surprised. 'No kidding—you've got class, Casey. Okay, come on.' He took her glass and put them both under the seat. 'We'll come back for those later.'

No, we won't, she thought, but said nothing. They passed within inches of Igor and his partner, and he looked at them both, and grinned, then bent to hear something the girl had whispered. His laugh followed them as they swirled away, doing a quickstep this time, Casey realised, in confusion.

The music had changed. Someone somewhere was putting on records, which were being relayed over a loudspeaker, and that someone was obviously choosing with a blindfold on, for the next one was 'The Teddy Bears' Picnic.' Slight confusion ensued, and during it Igor appeared, tapped the American on the shoulder and handed him the redheaded girl.

'She's been anxious to meet you,' he told Chuck, with a wink and something approaching a leer. 'I hope you speak French?' Then with a disarming smile at Casey, he added: 'I'd like to dance with my wife, if you don't mind.' He took hold of Casey, nodded pleasantly to the American who stood there clasping a startled redhead, and whirled Casey away from them.

'What did you do that for?' she said, bewildered.

Instead of answering, he pushed her down into the seat she had so recently vacated. She glared up at him. 'I didn't think anything could prise you two apart,' she said. He laughed.

'It was difficult, yes. But when a lady asks you to dance, what can you do?'

'I don't know. Ladies don't ask me,' she retorted.

He sat down beside her. 'You are angry at me dancing? When you go off with that young American Romeo? I only followed to make sure you were all right.'

'You didn't look as though you were,' she said.

'I was watching, never fear. I brought you, so you are with me. It is my duty to look after you.' Then his face changed. 'I had a reason for separating you.' He paused. 'This is difficult. Someone has just arrived. I saw them as I was dancing with Claudette.'

'Who?'

'Claudette——'

'No, not her. Who's arrived?'

'I promised not to say his name again tonight——'

'You don't mean—oh no!' She looked at him. 'Jack?'

'Yes. With Lucia and the other woman. I saw them coming along the gangplank.'

'What shall we do?'

'What do you want to do?'

'We can't leave, we've only just arrived——'

'It might be better.'

'Did you know they'd be here?' she said accusingly.

'No. How could I?'

'I don't know with you. You seem to know everything.'

'I swear I didn't. I brought you for another reason——' he stopped.

Casey suddenly didn't want to know what it was. She looked at him. 'I think you'd better take me home—I mean, back to the *château*.'

'As you wish.' He stood up. 'Come—they are in the saloon.' They edged their way along the deck, and then a strange thing happened. Casey paused as they passed the window of that main room, and, unable to help herself, looked in. Jack was there all right, standing with Lucia, her friend, and several more people, all obviously knowing one another. He had his arm around Lucia, he was clearly drunk, and he was laughing at something one of them had said. She saw Lucia look up at him smiling, and he bent and kissed her.

Casey felt sick. 'Let's go,' she whispered. Igor had seen it as well. He took her arm, and they reached the gangplank and went up it to the stone quayside. More people were arriving, noisy groups of chattering men and women pushing their way past them, laughing, talking—Casey held Igor's arm. Her sandals click-clacked along the pavements as they walked along in silence towards Igor's car.

He opened the door and helped her in, closed it, and went round to his own. Casey lay back in the seat and closed her eyes, hearing him start the engine, rev the motor up, and drive away from the yacht they had just left. So that was it. The marvellous party, finished before it had begun, and the evening ruined. There was a bitter taste in her mouth.

She opened her eyes, and looked around, then said: 'But this isn't the way home?'

'No, I know.'

'Where are we going?'

'Wait and see.' He looked briefly at her. 'I made you come, so you will have your evening out after all.'

Casey was too confused to care. The car climbed steadily, and she had a brief flash of panic as the town was left behind, and everything became dark, with only the headlights of the car lighting the way ahead. On and on, up and up, and the road now was narrower, no longer a busy main route, but in country, with only the occasional car going past.

'Igor,' she said quietly, 'please tell me where you're going.'

'To a restaurant I know, owned by a friend—a Russian—in a remote village. There we will eat—if you wish—or have a quiet drink, and then return home. That is all. Were you worried?'

'No.' It was the truth. She knew he had sensed her mood, and that his too was different. Something had happened tonight, and she wasn't sure what it was exactly, but everything had subtly and inexorably changed—and would never be the same again. There was no way of saying at which point it had occurred. There had been no flash of insight, of sudden awareness, just a gradual realisation of a shift at a certain level.

She saw houses, and lights far ahead, and he slowed his speed to a moderate level as they reached the village. And then she saw the long low building to their right, the ground packed with cars, lights winking out in welcome.

'We are here,' he said.

The atmosphere inside was quiet, in startling contrast to the party they had so recently left. People sat at tables in a large room, and the discreet clink of cutlery and glass mingled with the voices, and one or two looked round as they went in, then back to their meals, and white-coated waiters moved among the tables——

'Igor! *Mózhno, tovarich!*' A small roly-poly of a man detached himself from a group of people and came over to them, and hugged Igor delightedly, his round face beaming, chins wobbling with joy. She listened to them speaking in Russian for a minute or so, then Igor turned to her, took her hand, and said in French:

'Casey, I want you to meet Sergei Feodorov, a very good and old friend of mine. Sergei, this is Casey Cantrell.'

The Russian shook her hand, his blue eyes regarding her with pleasure. 'You are very welcome here, *mademoiselle*, very welcome.' She wondered if she would ever get her hand back, or if it would be intact, and it left her in no doubt about the sheer warmth of the man. 'Come, we will find you the best table. Franco—Emilio—table five for my friends.' He turned and led the way to a discreet and dimly lit corner of the large room where even as they reached it, a clean cloth was being laid.

'Now sit down. I will be back in one moment.' He waddled away, catching a waiter's arm, firing instructions rapidly, the waiter nodding:

'*Oui, monsieur, ah oui, tout de suite.*'

Then they were alone. Igor looked across the table at Casey, and grinned. 'Nothing is too much trouble for Sergei. You may have as much or as little as you want to eat or drink. And you will enjoy it. His chefs are superb.'

She looked round her at the crowded tables. 'I'm feeling better already—and quite hungry.'

'Good.' He nodded. 'That is what matters. If he joins us for a while, you will not mind, will you? I do not see him often—and he always has much to tell me.'

She smiled faintly. 'I don't mind if you speak in Russian, I like listening to it—though I don't understand a word.'

He laughed. '*Moy deeki gus.*'

She lifted her eyebrows. 'What?'

'Nothing.' He looked round as Franco—or was it Emilio?—came up with a bottle of wine.

'*M'sieur?* With M'sieur Feodorov's compliments.

He asks me to ask you if you will leave everything to him,' the dark Italian face creased in a smile. 'I think he goes to prepare something special for his friends.'

'Tell him we are in his hands completely.' Igor poured out the cool *rosé* wine as the waiter left them. 'Drink, Casey.' He raised his glass. '*Na zdorovye.*'

'*Na zdorovye.*' The warm atmosphere of cheer and friendliness washed round her, and she sipped the sparkling *rosé* wine and felt herself relax. There was something she had been going to ask Igor, but she couldn't remember what it was. What was it he had said? She couldn't remember that either. The bitter aftertaste of the party was vanishing rapidly. It would have been a mistake to have gone straight back to the *château*, feeling as she had. All that was being gradually washed away. Perhaps Igor knew. He always did.

CHAPTER TEN

It was several hours later, and Casey had just looked at her watch in astonishment. Surely it couldn't be one o'clock in the morning? The time had vanished, it seemed. Sergei, sitting beside her, chuckled.

'It is late, yes?'

'I was just wondering where the last three hours had gone—but now I know. I've enjoyed the meal very much, Sergei. And talking to you.' He was an excellent *raconteur*, she had spent more time listening than talking, enchanted with his tales of the life he had led, and of the occasionally hilarious existence of a *restaurateur*.

'It was my pleasure. I see Igor too seldom—you will come here again with him?'

She could hardly say no. A diplomatic lie was necessary. 'Of course. I'd love to.'

'Good—good,' he beamed. 'Ah, more liqueur?'

'Oh, please—well, thank you,' this as he ignored her protest and filled her glass, then his own. Then she remembered what it was Igor had said. She had a good memory for phonetics. Igor had left them minutes previously and would soon be back.

'Sergei, what does *moy deeki gus* mean?'

He repeated the words, frowning slightly, then chuckled. 'You are sure you have it right?'

'Well, I think so. It was something Igor said, and then the waiter came, and I forgot to ask him.'

'It means—"my wild goose", little one.' He laughed merrily. 'Is that what you are?'

She was confused. 'Well, it was just his little joke. Er—don't tell him I asked, will you? Then I can surprise him by my knowledge of Russian, can't I?'

'Of course. Ah, he is a good man, Igor. A fine man. He must not leave it so long next time, neglecting his old friends——' he raised his voice as Igor approached. 'I am telling Casey you neglect your old friends—you come again soon, you hear me?'

'I hear you, old friend,' Igor agreed easily, as he sat down, 'and so do the rest of your customers.'

'Pah!' Sergei filled Igor's liqueur glass. 'Drink up. They don't care, they are used to me. But you—you will return in two weeks, hey? It is my birthday.'

There was a brief silence, and Igor looked at Casey. Then: 'I promise I will be here. *And* I'll bring you a present.' He smiled.

I'll be here, he had said. Because he knew she wouldn't. 'Excuse me,' she said, 'no, don't get up, Sergei, I can get past,' she squeezed behind his chair and walked away steadily towards the ladies' powder room.

Sitting inside it, renewing her vanished lipstick, she looked at herself in the mirror. The sun had caught her, and her cheeks were pink. Or was that with all the wine she had drunk? Igor would come here again, alone, and the two old friends would talk and exchange jokes, as they had done this evening, and I'll be back home in London, she thought. She blotted her lips on a tissue, smoothed her hair, and stood up. And why do I suddenly feel so unhappy at that? she thought. Wild goose—wild goose. The words echoed in her head as she returned to the restaurant.

She fell asleep on the way home, but was not aware she had done so until she realised the car wasn't moving, and opened her eyes. 'Why have we stopped?' she asked. They were surrounded by trees, and could have been anywhere.

'We are nearly at the *château*,' Igor answered. 'I wanted to talk.'

'I'm very tired. Have I been asleep?'

'Yes. Casey, I did not know Jack would arrive at the party tonight. I wanted only for you to meet your friends—your kind of people—again.'

'I'm not sure if they are my kind of people,' she answered slowly. 'I've known Kim a long time, and I like her, but——' she stopped. She was remembering the restaurant, and Sergei—and the contrast between him and all the party guests. They were a world apart. 'But I'm not sure whether I'd class myself as her close friend.' She sighed. 'I'm sorry, I can't think straight. I had a wonderful evening with you and Sergei, far better than anything that could have happened at any party, but I am really tired.'

'I know. But sometimes, when you are tired, you can see things more clearly.' It was there, the subtle prickling of awareness and tension, the quiet under-currents flowing round them.

'Perhaps I do,' she answered quietly. She took off her engagement ring and put it in her bag. 'I know now what you knew all along. Jack and I aren't suited to each other.' She paused. 'Please—take me home.'

She heard him let out his breath in a deep sigh. 'Casey——' he began.

'Please, Igor.' Tears blurred her eyes. 'I—I don't want to talk. Not now.'

He gripped the steering wheel tightly, then: 'Very well, we will go.'

He started the engine, and as it moved, she saw that they had been in the drive—for the *château* suddenly appeared, and it was ablaze with light.

'My God, what——' Her pulse quickened, tears vanished. He increased speed, drove the last quarter mile or so in no time at all, stopped the car, and ran towards Boris, who was coming down the steps towards him. Casey ran after him, heart in mouth. Something had happened. She heard them talking as she reached them, and Igor turned to her.

'Get inside with Boris,' he said.

'What is it? What's happened?'

'Someone was here. He sent the dogs after him—I'm going after them.' She could hear the two dogs barking from somewhere in the woods, and caught his arm.

'Igor, wait! Let's get the police——'

'No, I know who it was. Get back inside——' he took something from Boris, and she saw that it was a gun. 'You have done well, my friend. But we won't need that. You can put it away.' He handed it back.

'He was trying to start a fire,' said Boris. 'At the back—he had laid a pile of old rags by the door, and there was a tin of petrol——'

Casey put her hand to her mouth. 'Jean Gallion,' she whispered.

'Yes.'

'He won't be back.' Igor looked at Boris. 'Take her in. Make coffee—but stay inside until I get back.'

Then he was off, running swiftly over the lawns towards the belt of trees. Casey looked at Boris wide-eyed. 'I must go——' she began.

'No.' He took her arm. 'I dare not let you. Come inside, quickly, please.'

'But he might need help——'

'He will manage. And he will have the dogs. Please —inside.' Shaking, she allowed him to lead her indoors, and he bolted the heavy door.

'I must go and see if everyone is safe upstairs,' she said.

'Then go. I will make coffee in the kitchen.' She saw that he was shocked, and trembling.

'Yes, do that, Boris. I'll be down in a minute.' She ran upstairs to the bedrooms where Claire and her family slept. All was well. But the next hour was sheer hell. All her tiredness had vanished in those few horrifying seconds when they had returned, and Casey paced the kitchen nearly demented with worry, her vivid imagination filling her mind with horrifying pictures of what might be happening to Igor. Time and time again she went to the window and looked out to the blackness. No sound, no movement.

Boris sat at the table, smoking endless cigarettes, and she made more coffee for them and poured it out. Then she went for the cognac and added a stiff measure of it to his coffee. 'Drink that, Boris,' she said. 'It will do you good.' In soothing him, she helped herself, but only slightly. She sat down, then jumped up again to go to the window. She pressed her forehead against the pane of glass, and prayed. She could not cry; she was numb with fear.

Then there came a banging on the back door, a scratching and whining, and she whirled round as Boris rose to his feet. Heart in mouth, she ran out of the kitchen, and flung the door open.

'Igor—oh, Igor!' Sobbing with relief, she put her arms round him, and pulled him in. The alsatians followed, tongues out, panting, but Casey had eyes only for the man who stood there soaking wet, dirty, a long cut down his cheek. The man, she had realised in the last endless hour, that she loved.

He looked at her. 'Get me a coffee, will you, Casey? I'm going to change.' He glanced down at his sodden clothes.

'Yes. Go quickly.' She watched him go, then caught Boris by the arm. 'He's safe,' she said unnecessarily. 'He's safe—thank God!' The relief on Boris's face was wonderful to see.

'Yes, yes,' he said. 'Coffee for him.' He walked

away as if the cares of the world had rolled off his shoulders, and Casey followed.

They waited and waited, and when fifteen minutes had passed, and the coffee had been bubbling away on the stove for what seemed ages, she said: 'I'm going to take it up to him.'

'Had I better not——' he began.

'No, let me,' she said quietly. 'You'd better go to bed, Boris.'

'Yes, I will. I will feed the dogs first. They deserve a reward.' He smiled faintly at her. Casey poured a beakerful of coffee, added cognac, and went quietly out.

She had to walk slowly lest she spill it, and when at last she reached Igor's door, she knocked and waited. There was silence from within.

She knocked again. 'Igor?'

'Come in.' He was standing by the window, clad in the black dressing gown, his clothes in a bundle on the floor. He didn't turn, and she went over to him.

'Igor, I've brought your coffee.' She touched his arm, and he turned, and she saw the deep pain in his eyes. Then, wordlessly, he took her in his arms.

'Hold me. Just hold me.' His voice was muffled, and he was trembling. She had never seen him like this, and she was filled with a sense of strength and peace as she held him in her arms, her hand at the back of his neck, standing on tiptoe so that his cheek could rest on hers.

'It's all right. Don't talk,' she whispered. And gradually he became still, and calmer. But still he held her as if he would never let her go. Then he gave a long, shuddering sigh. She stood back and smiled at him. 'Sit on the bed and drink your coffee.' She let him walk over, and then followed, handing him the coffee as she sat beside him.

He looked at her then. 'You are good for me,' he said quietly. 'I needed strength just then, and you gave it to me. I will tell you what happened.'

'You don't need to. In the morning will do.' She watched him take a deep swallow of the hot coffee, and he spluttered.

'Agh! What have you put in it?'

'Cognac. Doctor's orders—drink it all.'

He pulled a face. 'You are telling *me* what to do?'

'Yes,' she answered firmly.

He shrugged, drank the rest, and put the beaker down. 'You were right, doctor,' he said. Then he looked at her. 'He was in the lake,' he said. 'I followed the dogs barking and found him there. That is why my clothes are wet.' He put his hand up to his eyes. 'He was nearly dead. Had I not followed when I did, he would have drowned.'

'Oh *no*!'

'Yes. He was caught—his foot was caught in a trap under the water, at the lake edge. The dogs had chased him—and he had fallen in.' He looked down at his hands, and she saw the cuts and scratches there. 'Then I had to release his foot from the trap. I know now why Emil will not speak.'

'But——' she couldn't follow the swift change of subject. 'I don't understand——'

'He had placed the trap there, to try and catch one of the geese——'

'Oh no! How could anyone——'

'It is broken now. I smashed it with a stone. I thought tonight, when I went out, that I could have killed him. I was prepared to do—does that shock you?'

'Not any more,' Casey shook her head. 'And Emil had seen him do it—and had afterwards tried to remove it?'

'Yes. He told me that much as I carried him down to the village. He was talking wildly, half dead—but I knew it was the truth.' He took Casey's hand. 'I felt a dreadful pity for him. All the hate had gone. He is mentally sick.'

'What will happen to him now, after tonight here?' she asked quietly. The pressure of his hand on hers was reassuring. He was coming back to normal. The more he talked it out the better he would be.

'The doctor called the police before he treated him. He will go to prison, undoubtedly—but he will get treatment, I will see to that.'

'We'll have to tell Claire. But not yet. When she's stronger.'

'I know.' He looked suddenly very weary, the lines of strain showing on his face.

'Lie down and rest, Igor.'

He shook his head. 'No. I want to talk to you.'

'In the morning. It's nearly four o'clock. We must both get some rest——'

'If I say what I have to say now, it is better.' He looked at her, and what she saw in his eyes made her heart lurch in a crazy manner. 'You and Jack—you are finished?'

'Yes.' She was nearly asleep, the fatigue and delayed shock catching up with her suddenly. He touched her cheek gently.

'Go now, then, and sleep. Thank you for bringing me the coffee.' His concern showed in his eyes.

'You're all right? Your cheek—that scratch——'

'It is nothing.' She stood up and looked down at him sitting exhausted on the bed. 'Goodnight, Igor.'

'Goodnight, Casey.'

She went out and closed the door softly behind her.

No sooner had she climbed into bed than she was asleep, and when she awoke in the morning after a profound slumber of less than six hours, she felt much better. So many things had happened that she couldn't even begin to think about them. She washed and dressed and went into Claire's room. It was empty, as was Annette's cot. Apprehensive—surely nothing else could have happened?—Casey ran down to the kitchen to see Claire and the baby seated at the table with Boris. They were all eating.

Casey collapsed against the door in relief. 'Oh, Claire, you gave me a fright!' She looked at Boris, who gave a warning shake of the head. Claire knew nothing.

'I feel so much better. The children brought me

down and then went out,' Claire answered. 'I did not wish to wake you after your night out. Did you enjoy the party?'

'I had a lovely evening, yes, thanks,' Casey answered. 'Where's Igor?'

Boris looked at her. 'He is not up yet,' he said.

'Oh. Shall I take him coffee?'

'It is ready, yes.' As he made to get up, Casey said quickly:

'I'll pour it out. I'll be down in a minute for mine.' She filled a beaker, added milk, and went out of the room with it. Filled with concern, she knocked on Igor's door and waited. There was silence. Very quietly, she opened it, peeped in—and saw his bed empty.

'Igor!' Where had he gone? She put the beaker down on the chest of drawers, and his voice came from the doorway:

'I am here.' She whirled round, to see him fully dressed, carrying a towel. 'I was in the bathroom shaving when I heard you. I thought I would surprise you.'

'You gave me a fright. How are you?'

He walked over to her. 'I am fine—thanks to you, doctor.'

'I did nothing. You looked so exhausted when you came back. I was worried about you this morning.' She looked at him. The lines of fatigue had gone from his face; only the long scratch remained. She reached up to gently touch it. 'Poor Igor!'

He caught her hand and kissed the palm. Casey sighed. She had something to say, and it was going to be difficult. 'Igor,' she began, 'I've brought you coffee—and I want to talk to you.'

'Yes? So serious, Casey. What is it? Come, sit down and let me drink my coffee while we talk. You have had some?'

'No, not yet, I——'

'Then you shall share this with me. I too wish to talk to you—but the lady must speak first.' He sat on the bed and took a sip of his coffee.

'It's about this *château*,' she said. 'I've been thinking about it, and about everything——' she swallowed. This was not proving at all easy.

'Yes?' he prompted.

'And I've decided—that—I can hardly sell you something that doesn't really belong to me. You live here, and you love this place, that is obvious—and I'm sure you helped Uncle Edward a great deal.' She looked straight at him. 'What I'm trying to say is that —I want you to have my share. I give it to you gladly——' she paused. 'It should be quite easy, when we visit the lawyers, to sign it over——'

'Wait.' He put the beaker down. 'You would give me your half?' His voice had gone strangely husky. 'But why?'

'Because—oh, I've been trying to explain to you,' she said wretchedly. 'Do I have to spell it out?'

'Yes, I think you do.'

'I can't stay on here—too much has happened—

I'm all so mixed up. I just want to get back to London and——'

'But I don't want you to go, Casey.' He cupped her face in his hands. 'I want you very much to stay.'

'But it wouldn't be right—not now—not after all that has happened——'

'Do I not make myself clear? Or am I mistaken in what I have seen in your eyes when I held you?'

Her mouth trembled. 'I'm not sure what you——' she caught her breath, pulse beating fast. Then he bent his head and kissed her. Such a long, gentle, heart-melting kiss that turned her body to fire.

'I love you, Casey. I love you with all my heart, as no man has ever loved a woman before. From the very first moment I saw you—and perhaps before, since the beginning of time. I was waiting for you to come into my life. Without you now, there would be nothing, I know that. If you go, I will follow—it is as simple as that.' He stroked her cheek so very gently with his hand. 'Now,' he murmured huskily, 'am I making myself clear to you?'

She could hardly speak. 'I think—yes——' she smiled, and her soul was in her eyes. 'But if you want to tell me again, I think I could listen.'

He laughed softly. 'My wild goose. My very own wild goose. Yes, I will tell you again. Where shall I begin? I think I will begin when I first walked into the room downstairs to see you waiting for me, and I had not wanted to meet this English girl who was to share my home—and then I saw you, and something was stirring within me even then, but I resisted it, for you were nothing to me.' He lifted her hand to his face. 'But I was lost, very soon I was lost—and angry with you for daring to have a fiancé. I, who had not wanted a woman before, wanted you very much. And now I know that I need you as well. That is something hard for a man to say, to admit he needs someone. I have always been so strong—yet this morning you held me, and gave me my strength back. And I knew then that I could never let you go.' He kissed her again. 'So you see, *moy deeki gus*, that I will never let you escape me now. What do you have to say to that?'

'I think I'd like to hear some more,' she said slowly, mischievously.

'You would? Then of course you shall. But first——' he stood up, went to the door and closed it. 'That is better,' he said slowly, coming towards her. 'For what I have to say now is very private.' He sat down and drew her into his arms. 'I don't think lunch will be for quite a while,' he said. 'But I am not hungry for food. Are you?'

She smiled. 'No.'

Down in the kitchen, Boris took the coffee pot from the stove. There seemed no sense in wasting heat, and the coffee had been bubbling away for a long time. He began to pour himself another cup. There was no sense in wasting good coffee either. He smiled a little smile to himself. It looked as though he would be preparing lunch on his own.

Send coupon today for
FREE
Harlequin Presents
Catalog

We'll send you by return mail a complete listing
of all the wonderful Harlequin Presents novels
still in stock.

Here's your chance to catch up on all the
delightful reading you may have missed
because the books are no longer available at
your favorite booksellers.

Fill in this handy order form and mail it today.

Harlequin Reader Service
MPO Box 707,
Niagara Falls, N.Y. 14302

In Canada:
649 Ontario St.
Stratford, Ont. N5A 6W2

Please send me without obligation my FREE Harlequin
Presents Catalog.

NAME _____
(please print)

ADDRESS _____

CITY _____

STATE/PROV. _____ ZIP/POSTAL CODE _____

ROM 2147

Have you missed any of these best-selling Harlequin Romances?

By popular demand... to help complete your collection of Harlequin Romances

50 titles listed on the following pages...

Harlequin Reissues

Harlequin Reissues

Complete and mail this coupon today!

Harlequin Reader Service
MPO Box 707
Niagara Falls, N.Y. 14302.

In Canada:
649 Ontario St.
Stratford, Ont. N5A 6W2

Please send me the following Harlequin Romances. I am enclosing my check or money order for 95¢ for each novel ordered, plus 25¢ to cover postage and handling.

☐ 1282	☐ 1394	☐ 1481
☐ 1284	☐ 1397	☐ 1483
☐ 1285	☐ 1433	☐ 1484
☐ 1288	☐ 1435	☐ 1638
☐ 1289	☐ 1439	☐ 1643
☐ 1292	☐ 1440	☐ 1647
☐ 1293	☐ 1444	☐ 1651
☐ 1294	☐ 1449	☐ 1652
☐ 1295	☐ 1456	☐ 1654
☐ 1353	☐ 1457	☐ 1659
☐ 1363	☐ 1462	☐ 1675
☐ 1365	☐ 1464	☐ 1677
☐ 1368	☐ 1468	☐ 1686
☐ 1371	☐ 1473	☐ 1691
☐ 1372	☐ 1475	☐ 1695
☐ 1384	☐ 1477	☐ 1697
☐ 1390	☐ 1478	

Number of novels checked _____ @ 95¢ each = $_____

N.Y. and N.J. residents add appropriate sales tax $_____

Postage and handling $____.25

TOTAL $_____

NAME _____
(Please print)

ADDRESS _____

CITY _____

STATE/PROV. _____ ZIP/POSTAL CODE _____

ROM 2147